Mistletoe for the Sheikh

A Novel By

Annabelle Winters

Books by Annabelle Winters

The Curves for Sheikhs Series

Curves for the Sheikh
Flames for the Sheikh
Hostage for the Sheikh
Single for the Sheikh
Stockings for the Sheikh
Untouched for the Sheikh
Surrogate for the Sheikh
Stars for the Sheikh
Shelter for the Sheikh
Shared for the Sheikh
Assassin for the Sheikh
Privilege for the Sheikh
Ransomed for the Sheikh
Uncorked for the Sheikh
Haunted for the Sheikh
Grateful for the Sheikh
Mistletoe for the Sheikh
Fake for the Sheikh

MISTLETOE FOR THE SHEIKH

A NOVEL BY

ANNABELLE WINTERS

2018
RAINSHINE BOOKS
USA

Copyright Notice

Copyright © 2018 by Annabelle Winters
All Rights Reserved by Author
www.annabellewinters.com
ab@annabellewinters.com

If you'd like to copy, reproduce, sell, or distribute any part of this text, please obtain the explicit, written permission of the author first. Note that you should feel free to tell your spouse, lovers, friends, and coworkers how happy this book made you. Have a wonderful evening!

Cover Design by S. Lee

ISBN: 9781792109829

0 1 2 3 4 5 6 7 8 9

Mistletoe for the Sheikh

1

Sheikh Bawaar Al-Wakhrani put down the phone and clenched his fists. His knuckles were still bruised from punching the wall earlier, but the wall had been the loser in that battle. He thought about making another hole in the wall of his office, but then decided to hold his rage inside. Perhaps it would be useful later.

"Sheikh Bawaar, there is another phone call for you. It is your wife again," came his American assistant's high-pitched voice over the state-of-the art intercom system set up by the overpriced contractors who'd built this office in a suburb of Houston, Texas. This was supposed to be the base for all North American operations of the Sheikh's rapidly growing conglomerate company—a diversified corporation that owned businesses ranging from condoms to ice-cream. His wife had spent the last three years nagging him to set up shop in America so she could spend some time outside of their kingdom of Wakhrani, and finally the Sheikh had relented and done just that.

And now she had filed for divorce.

Divorce! A queen does not file for divorce from her king! A Sheikh does not grant divorces to his Sheikhas! If this were a hundred years ago, she would be tossed in a dungeon to await her fate of being buried up to the neck in the sand and stoned to death by the people of Wakhrani!

The Sheikh clenched his fist again as he stared at the black phone on his desk. A red light was blinking on it. His wife again. Now what did she want? Even after leaving him she thought she had the right to nag him like the succubus she was?

Bawaar laughed when he reminded himself that a succubus was a mythical entity that used sex to gain power over a man. That was not his wife. The last time he'd had sex with Renita it was like fucking one of those sex-dolls that just lies there on the bed, legs spread, eyes staring the ceiling. He hadn't touched her in months, and now even the thought made him sick. Had she picked up on his lack of interest and decided to pre-empt the inevitable break-up by asking for a divorce before he did? The woman had always been vain and insecure, even though she was a beauty in her own way.

But she can be a beauty for some other man now, the Sheikh thought as he exhaled slowly, acknowledging that in a way he was relieved. He knew he didn't love her, and he was certain she'd never loved him. Their marriage hadn't been completely arranged, but their meeting was indeed arranged by their families, and it had been virtually assumed that Bawaar and Renita would be married.

"But now it is over," the Sheikh said out loud, watching as the printer silently pushed out the divorce agreement Renita's lawyers had sent over via email. He flipped through the papers, grunted once, and then signed his name at the bottom. "Done."

"Sheikh Bawaar," came his assistant's voice over the phone. "You wife is on the—"

The Sheikh felt his anger rise so fast he almost tossed the phone across the room. But somehow he controlled himself and picked up the receiver, closing his eyes and wondering how many more times he'd have to endure her insults before she was gone from his life.

"I have signed the papers, Renita," he said, trying to sound as unperturbed as possible. "I am agreeing to whatever it is you asked for. The house in Switzerland. The flat in Paris. The houseboat in Amsterdam. Even the goddamn racehorse that you insisted we buy. Not to mention enough money to keep you fat and happy for the rest of your days."

Renita had never been fat, and in fact she had always been far too skinny for the Sheikh's private tastes. Still, Bawaar knew she'd always obsessed about her figure, and he couldn't help making the comment just to hurt her. It was cruel, he knew. But she was no better. He'd seen the perverse pleasure she'd gotten from insulting him by saying she was leaving him, as if it were her choice, as if she thought she could do better! Ya Allah, that woman! No substance whatsoever! Just false pride and fragile ego wrapped up in the finest silks!

The Sheikh swallowed hard and closed his eyes. He was self-aware enough to know that his own rage was largely because of the insult of what she was doing. The fact that she would be out of his life soon was a relief, perhaps even a joy! But the insult . . . ya Allah, that stung. A Sheikh does not have his women walk out on him! He kicks them out!

"I was thinking," came Renita's dull, lifeless voice over the phone, "that perhaps it was in poor taste to leave you just before the grand opening of your American offices. You have just hired almost a hundred people, and it is the time of the holidays in America. December is a holy month for both Christians and Muslims, and I believe there is a tradition for American companies to have Christmas parties. We should have one at the new offices. I will attend as your wife and Sheikha. We will make your new employees feel special and welcomed. And then we will make the divorce effective on the 1st of January. Yes?"

The Sheikh tightened his jaw as he looked down at the bruises on his left hand. He wanted to hit something again. Perhaps even someone. He grinned as he thought about the one time he'd flipped his wife over onto her stomach and spanked her bottom. She'd screamed like nothing on Earth, kicking at him and calling him a sadist, a madman, even a rapist! Bawaar had been shocked at the reaction, and he'd backed off from her after that occasion, a sense of both shame and anger building in him from that moment onward. Had that been the beginning of the end for them? Was it just a simple matter of sexual incompatibility? No chemistry? No physics? No spark? No energy?

"No," he said softly. "You wanted the divorce. I have granted the divorce. It is done, Renita. You are no longer welcome in my presence. You have lost all your royal privileges. Have a blessed Ramadan. Oh, and a Merry Christmas too. I will consider your suggestion of the Christmas party. It might be a good way to get to know my new American employees."

2

Queenie Quinn stared at the employee schedule posted above the time-clock. She blinked, rubbed her big brown eyes, and then stared again. Yup, it still said she had to work from 9 to 5 on Christmas Eve.

"That's nine at *night* till five in the *morning*! On Christmas Eve! That's Christmas morning!" Queenie said, her voice shaking as she stormed into the head janitor's office down in the basement of the shiny new office building that was the American headquarters of the Wakhrani Group. Queenie had no idea what the company did, and she didn't really care. All she knew was that she'd needed a job after moving down to Texas from Juno, Alaska, and this company was paying its freakin' janitors twenty-five dollars an hour!

Hell yeah, she'd thought when she'd gotten the job after a brief interview with the head janitor, a matronly woman who spoke excellent English with a thick Mexican accent. It was only after she started work that Queenie discovered that the title "Head Janitor" was a misnomer—there were no other janitors: It was just Queenie and her boss. And since Queenie was the newbie, she got stuck with all the crappy shifts.

"There is a Christmas party on December 24th. It is mandatory for all employees, and it will go late into the night. Someone will have to clean up afterwards. And I will be in Church starting midnight on the 24th," Ms. Head Janitor had said, shrugging as she looked up from her desk in the spotless closet that was her office.

"Well, I wanna go to church too," Queenie grumbled. "And by Church I mean my bed. You can't ask me to work all night on Christmas Eve! It's inhumane! This is America, dammit! Not the Middle Eastern shithole that our CEO is from. And besides, if this freakin' Christmas party is mandatory, why aren't I invited as a guest instead of the goddamn help?"

Ms. Head Janitor had sighed and taken off her glasses. She shrugged and made a face that communicated some mix of amusement and annoyance. "I am just the help too, Ms. Quinn. This is the job, and if you don't like it, you can leave. Any other complaints can be addressed directly with Mister Bawaar, the CEO. I have heard he has an open door policy for all employees. If you are insulted that you have not been invited to the Christmas party, then feel free to take it up with him."

"Maybe I will," Queenie muttered, trying to turn on her heel. But she was wearing standard issue steel-toed shoes with heavy rubber soles, and they just made a squeaking noise on the polished tile, making her moves feel ridiculous.

She walked out of the office, glancing about to make sure no one was around before reaching back and pulling at the dark blue overalls that were riding up her butt. She hated this uniform. It made her butt look enormous—which, granted, wasn't hard to do since she did in fact have a sizable ass. But dumpy blue overalls didn't help.

Twenty-five bucks an hour plus an overnight shift-premium did help, though. Yup, that makes up for a lot of sins, Queenie told herself as she finally calmed down and reminded herself why she was doing this. She'd left Alaska because she hated the cold, hated the isolation, and hated feeling like her career options were limited by being in a small town in an out-of-the-way state. At least that was what she told anyone who asked. And she'd picked Texas because it was warm, big, and its cities were large and crowded. As for the job . . . well, she'd picked the job because it paid well and gave her a chance to figure out what she *really* wanted to do in life.

"Of course, I shoulda figured that out ten years ago, when I was still in my twenties," she told herself as she filled a mop-bucket and rolled her cart out to the service elevator toward the back of the building. "But nooo . . . Miss Queenie Quinn spent her twenties flitting in and out of colleges and relationships, in no particular order. And so now Miss Queenie Quinn is in her thirties, still single, with a bunch of unrelated college credits but no degree. Oh, and she's a janitor who has to work on Christmas Eve!"

Stop it, Queenie told herself as she felt the sinking feeling that had plagued her when she was younger, sensed the edges of the dark emotion that used to take over during the long, cold Alaskan winters, when the sun never shone too bright but never set either. Yeah, just fucking stop it. You aren't going back to that place. Not that physical place, and certainly not that mental place.

"Is there place for two in here?" came a deep, heavily accented voice that broke through her melancholy daydream.

Queenie glanced up from her mop-bucket, realizing with surprise that she had to crane her neck all the way up just to look into the man's eyes, he was so damned tall. And broad. And muscular. And goddamn he smelled nice! Like some kind of wild herbs that she was sure were expensive as hell. And shit, were those his eyes or emeralds?! So green! So intense! So focused . . . focused on her! OMG!

"Um," she said, blinking and glancing down, unable to find the confidence to hold the eye contact for any longer. She felt fat and unattractive in her blue overalls, and she wondered if she smelled bad too. Hell, her breath probably still smelled like onions from the three delicious breakfast burritos she'd gobbled before work. Damn that taco-truck that stopped in the parking lot every morning! Just don't burp in his face, Queenie, she told herself as she said, "Um," again because she couldn't think of any other words.

"Are you meditating?" he said, stepping into the elevator with her and her mop-bucket.

"What?" said Queenie, panicking when she realized that yes, she did smell like onions.

"Aum," said the man, smiling and folding his hands. "That is the word sages and mystics chant when they seek enlightenment through meditation."

"Um," Queenie said again, her face turning bright red like that salsa in her darned breakfast burrito. "I mean, no. I wouldn't know where to begin seeking enlightenment." She stared down at her bucket of soapy water, then at the man's shoes. "Nice shoes," she said without thinking. "Must be hard to keep them this clean and shiny."

And just as she said it the elevator bumped to a stop and the mop-bucket jumped from the impact and Queenie, who was nonchalantly leaning on the mop, trying to look cool and collected, felt her weight slam the bucket right into the man's shin.

He grunted and frowned just as the soapy water spilled over the edge of the yellow bucket, all over his shiny leather shoes.

"Ya Allah," he muttered, stepping back and raising his feet one at a time, gracefully tapping each foot on the floor as the suds rolled off the beautiful black leather. "My shoemaker will have a fit. These are the third pair I have ruined this month."

Queenie was too busy pulling out massive quantities of paper towels from the roll on her cart to listen closely, but somehow his words registered—as did his sublime accent: Middle Eastern and smooth, with a hint of European polish. As far as she could tell, anyway. What the hell did she know about polish?

"Oh, God," she said, getting down on her knees and beginning to furiously dry his shoes with the paper towels. "I'm so, so sorry! I can't even . . . oh, shit, I'm so sorry!"

The man was quiet, and Queenie heard the metal doors of the elevator slowly close again since no one had stepped in or out. She kept rubbing his shoes, puzzled by the man's sudden silence. Then she looked down at herself and realized the front of her overalls were hanging open, and her cleavage was pretty much hanging out there.

Queenie had a big butt and a round belly, but she

also had boobs, that much she knew. She was about to cover up, but her hands were soaked from the paper towels and she didn't want to get the suds all over herself. So she just kept her head down and stuck with the shoe-shining, slowly realizing that the man's breathing had become heavy and labored.

She glanced up with her eyes, and then gasped when she realized her head was at the level of his crotch . . . his crotch which was so filled out that there was no doubt he was erect like a goddamn animal in heat right then. A flash of her own heat suddenly whipped through Queenie as she stayed down on her knees knowing full well the man was staring right down at her.

What are you doing, she asked herself as she felt wetness between her legs, dizziness between her ears, fuzziness in her vision. She was aroused, plain and simple, and so was this guy.

And then she saw his wedding ring.

And at the same time she put it together that although she'd never met him, this must be the CEO. How many other well-dressed men with Middle-Eastern accents were getting into elevators at eight in the damned morning in the office?

This is my boss. My married boss. My married boss with a goddamn hard-on and ruined shoes.

"You can stop," the man said quietly, and when she looked up at him she saw that his face was flush, his eyes narrowed, some of that focus seemingly lost, as if he'd been in a daze. He blinked twice, and she wondered if he was embarrassed for staring down at her cleavage while she crouched there on her knees, her head lined up with his crotch.

Nope. He isn't embarrassed at all, Queenie realized as she stood up as gracefully as she could. He knew that I knew my cleavage was on full display, and he was shamelessly looking. Which means he probably thinks I'm a whore or a slut, parading my tits around the office for the boss's viewing pleasure. Oh, shit, what a start to my career in janitorial services.

"You are the janitor?" he said, taking a breath and smiling.

Queenie nodded, glancing down at his shoes and then up into his green eyes. God, he was handsome. Handsome and married. A terrible combination. She wasn't going there again. Nope. She wasn't that woman. She'd ruined one marriage already, and she wasn't going to ruin another.

"I'm sorry about the shoes," she said. "I can apologize to your shoemaker if you like. Though wouldn't he be happy to sell you another pair? More money for him, right?"

The man laughed, his green eyes twinkling. "It is not the money. It is the time. My shoes are handmade, and each pair takes twelve months to create."

"Twelve months for a pair of shoes? I want that job," Queenie said, half smiling, half frowning.

The man laughed again, his gleaming white, perfectly aligned teeth on full display as if in response to her booby-show. "Perhaps my shoemaker will take on an apprentice. You will have to move to the kingdom of Wakhrani, though. And if you think Texas is hot, you are most certainly not prepared for the desert, I assure you."

"I moved here *for* the heat," Queenie said, running her hands though her long brown hair, only realizing her hands were still soapy when she felt the suds get into her tresses. "Oh, shit, I'm a moron," she said, frowning as she reached for the roll of paper towels so she could dry her hair.

But she'd used up the entire roll, and now she had soap in her hair and nothing to dry herself with. Onions on her breath, suds in her hair, ruined shoes . . . what else could go wrong?

"This is not your day, is it?" said the man softly, and Queenie gasped when he stepped close to her, whipping out a black silk handkerchief with one hand, sliding his other hand gently around the back of her neck. "It is all right. I have had a rough day as well. Come here. I will repay the favor."

Queenie almost swooned as she inhaled deep of the man's scent. She barely came up to his chest, and from this close she could clearly see his massive pectorals through his white linen shirt which had the top two buttons undone.

"Repay the favor, huh?" she said as she took in the sight of his beautiful chest. "Tit for tat."

She felt his hand tighten around the back of her neck, his chest muscles flexing as his body stiffened from the laughter that rocked his powerful body. She went bright red when she realized what she'd said without thinking, and then suddenly they were both laughing, the boss and the janitor, the man and the woman, Queenie and the king.

"Sheikh Bawaar of Wakhrani," he said, finally letting go of her, his fingers caressing the back of her neck as he pulled his hand away.

"Queenie Quinn of . . . Alaska, I suppose," she said, blinking as she tried to come to terms with what had just happened between them. It was nothing, really. But in a way it was also something. Shit, it was definitely something. "And I know who you are, of course."

"I am embarrassed to say I do not know who you are, though," said the Sheikh. "I take pride in knowing all my employees, and I consider it a failure that I did not know your name before today."

"Well, I've only been here a few days," said Queenie, fighting the urge to touch her hair again. "And I'm the janitor. No reason you should know my name."

"I can think of two reasons I should know your name," said the Sheikh as he glanced down at her, his gaze resting on her chest for a moment before he blinked.

"Excuse me?" Queenie said, her mouth hanging open as she wondered if she should be offended or thrilled. "What the hell does that mean?"

The Sheikh blinked again, his brown face darkening as the color rushed to his cheeks. "No, that is not what I meant! Ya Allah, I am not thinking straight today!"

"Me neither," Queenie said, shaking her head and smiling. Just then the elevator doors opened again, and she took a breath and glanced out into the empty second-floor hallway. "Anyway, I think this is where you get off. Sorry about the shoes."

The Sheikh cleared his throat, his jaw tightening as he tried to stifle another laugh. Queenie frowned before closing her eyes and wincing when she realized what she'd just said: "This is where you get off?" Really? Was she in a low-budget porno movie? The boss and the curvy janitor? Soap suds and mops with long shafts?

"I will tell you what my shoemaker says about taking on an apprentice," the Sheikh called out as the elevator doors slowly closed on their first meeting. "Perhaps you could be the tester. Come up with creative ways to destroy his work."

"That I could do," said Queenie, feeling a warm tingle go through her as she gazed into his eyes and felt that sense of connection again. "I'm good at destroying things."

"I will see you at the Christmas party, yes?" he said just as the doors closed.

Queenie sighed when she remembered that she'd be at the Christmas party, but in her blue overalls and with her mop bucket. "Sure," she said to the metal doors. "Sure. I'll be here on Christmas Eve."

3
CHRISTMAS EVE

"Why are you here?" said the Sheikh, blinking at he stared at her. "I thought I made it clear you are not welcome here, or anywhere in my presence."

Renita smiled as she walked into the open lobby on the top floor of the office building. The walls had been decorated with snowflakes, red-and-green tassels, cutouts of Santa, and other miscellaneous Christmas-themed ornaments. In the corner by the floor-to-ceiling windows stood a Christmas tree, fully decorated with lights and stars. Every employee had showed up, and the room was crowded and loud, with people sampling from the lavish buffet, downing drinks from the open bar, and excitedly talking about the stack of neatly wrapped presents, each with an employee's name on it.

"Is there a gift with my name on it, dear husband?" said Renita as she walked around the room, that plastic smile still on her long brown face. She wore a red gown, fitted to her slender body, taken in tight around the waist and beneath her breasts.

The Sheikh could tell she was wearing a push-up bra that was heavily padded, and although the sight of Renita made him sick, his mind immediately went back to that meeting with Queenie Quinn—who most certainly did not need a push-up bra or any sort of augmentation. She was all woman, and as the Sheikh thought back to that moment in the elevators, he wished he had just followed his instincts and taken Ms. Quinn right there and then, against the metal walls of the elevators.

Suddenly his mind clouded over, and the Sheikh felt his cock harden at the thought of that janitor on her knees before him, her top opened out, her full lips just inches from his swollen cock. Did she do that on purpose? Was she tempting him? Was she hoping he'd unzip, grab her head, and push his cock down her throat? Ya Allah, he should have done it! He was king, boss, CEO, goddamn master! He should have taken that woman and satisfied his need. Perhaps he would be better prepared to handle whatever it was Renita had planned for this unexpected showing at the Christmas party.

He heard giggles and claps from his left, and when he looked he saw some of his employees cheering on a couple who were standing beneath a sprig of mistletoe.

"You gotta kiss now," someone called to them. "That's the rule. You're caught beneath the mistletoe."

"Kiss, kiss, kiss!" squealed someone else.

Soon everyone was hooting and hollering, and the Sheikh watched as the man and woman went bright red and then smacked each other hesitantly on the lips before hurriedly stepping away from the mistletoe. Bawaar couldn't help but smile at how embarrassed the two seemed to be, and he shook his head when he remembered that despite all its freedoms and the overtness of sex in movies and advertisements, American society still had this strange, almost hypocritical conservativeness when it came to interaction between men and women, especially in the workplace.

He sighed as the red-faced couple moved away from beneath the mistletoe, and then shook his head again when he saw how everyone else took care to keep their distance from the green-and-red plant as if it were poisonous. Ya Allah, perhaps he needed to set an example for his staff here. Let them know that it was all right for a man and woman to express what nature had put inside them: The need to touch, the need to love, the need to damned well *fuck*!

Bawaar blinked as he felt a strange combination of anger and arousal rise up in him. It had been a problem in the past, and indeed, he'd suspected that Renita had always been slightly afraid of him in the bedroom. Perhaps that was why she had always shut down.

Regardless, he thought as he smiled cordially at his wife before reminding himself that she was his *ex*-wife now—his ex-wife who was most certainly not here to open a goddamn present or kiss him beneath the mistletoe! She was here for a reason, and when the Sheikh saw the tall, blonde, long-haired man walk in behind her and slip his arm around her waist, he knew at once what the reason was:

Humiliation. A slap in the face. A public show that she was moving on, and that it was her choice to move on.

"Bawaar, this is Anders Van Hosen," Renita announced, her voice loud enough for them to hear her back in Austria—or wherever the hell this European male bimbo was from. "Of the Van Hosen family."

"Considering you introduced him as Anders Van Hosen, it follows that he is from the Van Hosen family," said the Sheikh coldly, doing his best not to take the bait even though he could feel his anger simmering. He could not let it rise to a boil, he knew. That would only give Renita what she wanted: To rile him up into a jealous rage, show the world that he wasn't in control of anything, let alone himself.

Of course, jealousy had nothing to do with the rage bubbling up in the Sheikh. He was simply upset at the insult, the very audacity of this woman showing up with some blonde underwear model. He couldn't care less about how many men Renita was fucking—hell, she could be doing the entire German national soccer team and Bawaar would just raise a glass and congratulate her. But she needed to do it in private. Off the radar. This display was tasteless, unbecoming of a person of her stature. It was not the behavior of a queen.

And so you need to behave like a king in response, the Sheikh told himself as he stepped forward and shook the man's hand, almost crushing the man's bones with his powerful grip. He felt a perverse satisfaction when he saw Mister Van Hosen wince, felt the European stud try to pull his hand away before the Sheikh destroyed it. He looked into the man's pale blue eyes, and then he let go and glanced back at Renita.

"Enjoy the party, you two," he said. Then he glanced at the mistletoe and winked at Anders. "Careful you don't step under there, or else you will have to kiss her in public. It has been a while, but if I remember correctly, she tastes like camel milk that has been left out in the sun."

The Sheikh clenched his fist when he saw Renita turn bright red, her mouth opening wide in feigned horror. He almost kicked himself for making that comment, knowing he'd said it loud enough for several people to hear. He'd made a mistake. He'd sunk down to her level. She'd dragged him down with her. Made him lose his cool, compromise his composure.

He blinked as he glanced around the room, wondering if already rumors were spreading through the office like wildfire. This whole CEO thing was fairly new to the Sheikh. He'd been a king for some time now, and he was very good at running a country. He hadn't been a boss for long, though—and certainly not in America, which was still a foreign country to him despite his familiarity with its people and culture.

Suddenly he felt a strange vulnerability as he saw a couple of his employees covering their mouths and whispering to one another as they glanced at the Sheikh, then at Renita and her blonde boy-toy. Ya Allah, was he seriously worried about office gossip?! He was a *king*! This was beneath him!

He spun around and glared at Renita, once again doing his best to keep the simmering rage under control. For a moment he considered grabbing her by the hair and flipping her over his knee right in front of everyone, spanking her skinny bottom beneath the Christmas tree just to show his employees that their boss was also a king who did not take insults lightly, a Sheikh who punished insolence and defiance his own way, no matter what country he was in.

He almost laughed at the image of himself doing that. The look on Renita's face as he ripped off her red dress and showed the world her bony bottom and carefully shaved pussy! Ya Allah, it would be priceless! Of course, chances were he'd be arrested, and without a doubt Renita would press charges. But that wasn't why the Sheikh knew he would never do such a thing. It wasn't fear of charges or accusations of assault. It was simply that the thought of seeing her naked again disgusted the Sheikh.

Still, he needed something to save face here, Bawaar thought as he rubbed his stubble and began to pace the room, just like he always did when he retreated into the solitude of his mind, the fortress of his thoughts. The live band had started playing, and Renita was dancing now, having Anders Van Hosen twirl her around like they owned the place. Of course, she was looking directly at the Sheikh, and everyone in the room could see that. What the hell was wrong with this woman?! He'd given her everything she wanted in the divorce! Why did she feel the need to invade his space, humiliate him in front of his new employees, insult him in public?

Again the rage bubbled up, and this time the Sheikh let it come. To hell with it, he thought. I am angry, and I want to strike back. If she wants public drama, I will give it to her. People are talking anyway, and so I might as well go all in, get down in the dirt with her and win at her game. I am more than capable of it. I can win at anyone's game, yes?

Bawaar stopped pacing suddenly, frowning as he felt all eyes on him. He blinked and looked around the room. Sure enough, every single employee was staring at him, most of them smiling, a couple of them nudging one another, one or two of them hesitantly whispering and pointing toward him. What, was he drooling? So he'd passed an off-the-cuff remark to his ex-wife who'd showed up just to insult him. So what? He was a goddamn king! He did not make apologies! What was the big deal anyway? Why was everyone staring at him like that.

The whispers slowly got louder, and finally someone plucked up the courage to shout, "Kiss!" to the Sheikh. Soon others joined in, and finally the entire room was hooting and howling, pointing above the Sheikh's head and shouting, "Kiss! You gotta kiss her now!"

The Sheikh turned in confusion, not sure what was happening. He looked up, and a chill ran through him when he saw that while pacing he'd ended up right beneath that hanging mistletoe. Then he whirled around, and the chill turned into a flash of heat that blindsided him with such power the Sheikh almost fell to his knees.

Because right there, right behind him, right beneath that same damned mistletoe, was Queenie Quinn, dressed in blue overalls, broom and dustpan in her hand, bent over as she swept up some crumbs from a spill.

She stood up just as the Sheikh turned, and then he was facing her, the entire room cheering them on. The CEO and the janitor. The Sheikh and the cleaning-lady. The king and . . . Queenie.

"Ya Allah," muttered the Sheikh, his green eyes lighting up when he looked into her big brown orbs that were widening as she realized what was happening . . . and what he was going to do.

"Um . . ." she whispered, taking a step back away from him. "Um . . . I don't think . . ."

"It is a tradition, is it not?" said the Sheikh, reaching out and grabbing her by the wrist, pulling her against his body, and then slipping his other arm around her ample waist.

"Well, yeah, but . . . I mean, it's OK if we don't. I mean, I'm just the . . . the . . ." she stammered, her eyelids fluttering as the Sheikh felt his cock rise just from being so close to her curves.

"You are perfect," he whispered, not sure if he meant that this was the perfect comeback to Renita's little act or if it was just straight-up perfect all around. Perfection, pure and simple. This woman. Her eyes. Her curves. And the moment. Pure perfection. A goddamn Christmas miracle. "Just perfect."

And then, with the room shouting and clapping, his ex-wife gaping and gasping, the broom and dustpan watching in silence, the Sheikh leaned in and kissed her, right on the mouth, hard and with authority.

Hallelujah, he kissed her.

4

She felt his arm tight around her waist like it belonged there, her body snug against his like her curves had been designed for his muscle. Every part of him felt hard and taut against her . . . every part of him except his lips. His lips felt soft and smooth, even though he'd kissed her hard and deep, his tongue pushing her lips open and driving inside her mouth before she understood what the hell was happening.

"What's happening?" she gasped as she broke from the kiss but was unable to break from his grasp. The Sheikh was holding her tight against him, looking down into her eyes. He's holding me like I'm his, she thought in that moment. Am I his now?

And then suddenly the moment was over and a new one had begun.

"We are not even divorced yet, and here you are kissing another woman right in front of me, in front of the entire world! Ya Allah, what have I done to deserve this treatment, Bawaar!" Renita howled, touching her forehead like she was an actress in a 1940s melodrama. "Have I not been a good wife? Did I not do my duty? Did I not . . . satisfy you, my husband?"

Queenie blinked and backed away from the Sheikh in horror, turning to the tall, thin woman in the red gown and makeup. This was his wife?! And he'd kissed her right in front of her and everyone else?! No way. This was not happening. She was *not* getting involved in some psychodrama unfolding between a married couple. Been there. Done that. And it had not ended well . . . not for anyone!

"OK, I need to . . . um . . . yeah," Queenie said, feeling the color rush to her face as she pointed at the dustpan and broom, both of which had clattered to the floor unnoticed in the confusion. "I should just . . ."

"I believe you missed a spot," declared Renita, raising an eyebrow and pointing directly at the Sheikh. "The dirt is right there, standing and staring like the sex-maniac he is. Though I do not think your dustpan will be able to handle that level of filth. Good luck. Do not say I did not warn you." Then Renita's sand-colored eyes narrowed, and she deliberately eyed Queenie up and down, her gaze resting on Queenie's bosom for a moment before moving down to her wide hips and then back up to her eyes. "Though perhaps you are well-made to handle Bawaar's filth, you American whore. Home-wrecker. Slut."

Queenie almost choked as she tried to understand what in God's name was unfolding here. This woman was either completely insane or else Queenie had inhaled too many cleaning products in the janitor's office and now she was hallucinating. Yup, that was it. Ammonia, Lysol, and freakin' Windex. Who needed LSD?!

"This is between you and me, Renita," she heard the Sheikh growl from behind her. Queenie could feel his anger, hear it in his voice, and for some reason it made her heart leap, made her think she was protected, she was safe, she was . . . his? "Do not insult someone you do not even know. It is one thing to insult me—ya Allah, I am used to that by now. But—"

"Insult?! What do you know about insults?!" Renita screamed, and Queenie took a step away from this madwoman who seemed on the one hand completely in control and on the other hand unhinged as all hell.

But the Sheikh had calmed down, and he stepped between Queenie and Renita. "Stop it, Renita. No one is fooled by your act. You were a terrible actor in bed, and you are equally bad when you are standing upright. Now take your European co-star in this little staged drama and get the hell off my property or I will have you thrown out on your bony arse."

"Act? Co-star? Drama? Have you no shame, Bawaar?" said Renita, her face suddenly going calm, her eyes going cold in a self-satisfied way that sent a chill through Queenie. "Anders is the head of Van Hosen Security. I hired his firm to protect me since my *husband* the*Sheikh* has declared that I no longer deserve to be protected by Wakhrani Secret Service. Me! The Sheikha!" She paused and swallowed, her gaze moving across the room before resting on the Sheikh, her expression showing faint triumph, as if she was getting to the finale of her little act. Or big act, Queenie couldn't quite tell. All she knew was that this bitch was good, and Queenie had best stay out of the goddamn way. She wasn't getting in the middle of whatever this was. Kings, queens, Sheikhs, Sheikhas? Nope. She was just the cleaning lady, and she needed to keep her head down and slip away offstage.

Queenie took a step to her left, eyeing the broom and dustpan and wondering if she should just leave it there and quietly exit the room. But then she looked at the Sheikh, saw the way he was standing there fearless and alone, every set of eyes on him.

Yeah, he's fearless, but he's also alone and vulnerable in this, she realized. He's been blindsided by this woman. Who knows whether they're officially divorced or not, but I can tell he isn't *with* her anymore—at least not in his heart. Perhaps he's never been with her in his heart.

Queenie saw the slightest of flinches in the Sheikh's stoic expression, and she somehow knew that no one besides her had seen it. Suddenly she felt like she knew him. Like they were connected. Like she understood him in a way that no one else did.

And so Queenie held her ground. She stayed silent, but she didn't move. She stood by his side, waiting for Renita to deliver the knockout punch, whatever it was. Somehow she knew she was already a part of this. She thought back to that chance encounter in the elevator, that second meeting beneath the mistletoe. A Christmas Miracle? Or was this the Nightmare before Christmas?

"That is not true, and you know it," came the Sheikh's voice, steady and even. "I never refused you the services of Wakhrani Security. In fact I was told you sent your bodyguards away last week, choosing to hire your own private security." He glanced at Anders Van Hosen and rolled his eyes. "With the bill coming to me, I should add."

"That is only right," Renita said, her lips tightening into a thin smile as she folded her long arms across her chest. "Because he is not just protecting me. He is also protecting the heir of Wakhrani. Our unborn child, Bawaar." She sighed, raising her eyebrows and touching her lip in a move that had clearly been rehearsed. "Tell me, Great Sheikh. If our child is born after we are divorced, does it mean I will be giving birth to a bastard?"

Queenie stared at Renita as she felt the Sheikh stiffen beside her. The room had gone dead silent. Not even a whisper emerged from the shocked onlookers. Even the band had stopped in awe of the madness being played out on center stage.

And then the Sheikh spoke.

"Out," he said. "Everyone. Everyone in the goddamn room. You too, Renita. Out. Now. *Now!*"

Queenie watched in stunned silence as the entire room slowly emptied. Not a single employee dared to let out even a murmur, and Queenie was certain several of them were actually holding their breath, afraid to make a sound in the Sheikh's presence.

In moments the room was empty, the faint clicking of the blinker on the Christmas lights the only discernible sound. Renita had left too, Queenie suddenly realized, even though it seemed odd that she would walk away after dropping that news out there. Had that always been her plan? Or was even that stoic queen scared of the Sheikh when he took command of the room?

The door at the far end closed with a soft thud, and it took Queenie a moment to realize that if she was watching the door close, seeing the Christmas tree stare back at her, hearing the Sheikh's deep but controlled breathing, it meant that shit, she was still here! Still in the room!

She glanced down at her feet in those steel-toed monstrosities that made her feel like Mrs. Frankenstein, frowning as she wondered why she hadn't left the room. Had the Sheikh even noticed? Had *anyone* noticed? Was a janitor so much a part of the background that no one could even see her anymore? Or was this truly a dream, her dream, which meant she had to be here or else all of it would go *poof* and disappear!

But then she felt the Sheikh's eyes upon her, and although her body shuddered and her knees trembled, she turned to him and glanced up into his green eyes. If this is my dream, she thought as she felt the Christmas lights blink at her—or perhaps wink at her—then I can do anything I want, and if it gets too weird, I'll just pinch myself and wake up!

Since when have you been able to control your dreams, you moron, she thought as Bawaar turned his full attention to her, his green eyes focused on her in a way that made her shift on her feet.

"Why are you still here?" he asked.

Queenie blinked and shrugged. "I have no idea," she finally said, half-turning toward the door but not taking a step. She glanced at the floor absentmindedly, wondering why her damned feet weren't moving, why she was feeling hot under those blue overalls, why those Christmas lights suddenly seemed like warning flashers. And had the damned Christmas music started to play again even though the band was gone? Had there ever been a band? What was going on?

"You do realize you are still standing beneath the mistletoe," came his voice from somewhere to her left, perhaps from above her. "And since it is a tradition, I must uphold it."

Queenie glanced up and saw the mistletoe in the archway above her. Then she felt the Sheikh's shadow fall across her, smelled his scent as he approached. Suddenly her feet came under her control again, and she took two steps back, moving out from beneath the mistletoe as she watched this king in his maroon fitted tuxedo approach.

"Are you crazy?" she whispered. "After what just happened? After what your wife said? After the news that she's . . . OK, you know what? There's no way. No. Stop. I said *no!*"

The Sheikh stopped just inches away from her, his lips so close to her face she could feel his warm breath on her smooth forehead. She felt him breathe deep, like he was trying to control himself, to hold himself back from taking what he wanted.

Queenie told herself she should take a step back. Hell, she should turn on her heels and run like hell, get away from this madness that was threatening to suck her in! But once again she was frozen in place, looking up into the Sheikh's eyes, that Christmas music sounding extraordinarily loud, almost booming.

"She is not my wife anymore," he said softly, reaching out and touching her hair gently. "And regardless of whether what she said is true, she will never be my wife again. I am single. It is Christmas Eve. We are alone in a room, standing beneath the mistletoe. And I am going to kiss you, unless you can think of a damned good reason why I should not."

Queenie blinked as she looked up into his eyes. He seemed almost a foot taller than her, broader than any man she'd been this close to. He could easily overpower her, she realized, and there was a part of him that wanted to do just that, she could tell. She could see the way he was taking deep breaths to control himself, clenching his left fist as the fingers of his right hand tightened in her hair. He's just looking for a release, Queenie thought, not sure if she was relieved or indignant. She couldn't deny the attraction, but neither could she deny that it would be pretty darned stupid to act on it in this messed-up, volatile situation with melodramatic, possibly pregnant, ex-wives and European security guards and a hundred office workers standing outside the door!

Oh, shit, Queenie thought as she pictured the scene if she walked out the door into the hallway right now. There'll be like a hundred people standing out there, whispering and wondering what the hell *she* was doing alone with the Sheikh all this time! Then she wondered if anyone would even remember she was in there or if the janitor in the blue overalls would just fade into the background, get erased from their collective memories. What would they say when they told the story to their friends? Would they remember her face? Was she a part of the story or just a prop: interchangeable, replaceable, disposable?

"I can think of a hundred reasons why you shouldn't kiss me again," Queenie heard herself saying, her own voice sounding surprisingly strong as it cut through that horrendous Christmas music.

"Well, you had better start listing them," he said, smiling as he leaned closer. Suddenly this felt like it was just the two of them alone in an elevator, alone in the world, alone in the universe. "And perhaps you will strike upon one that I actually give a damn about."

Queenie gasped as the Sheikh kissed her hard on the mouth and then pulled back. She staggered as the blood rushed through her body, electricity surged up and down her back, her buttocks tightened, her thighs flexed, her nipples stiffened all at once. Did that really just happen?

"Go on," he said, kissing her again and pulling back once more. "I am listening."

"Well," said Queenie, fluttering her eyelids as the words somehow kept coming even though she felt like she'd slipped from a dream into a daze into a full-on hallucination. "For one, your ex-wife just said she's pregnant with your child."

The Sheikh grunted. "It is usually a fifty-fifty chance that anything Renita says is a lie. But even if that is true, why is it wrong for me to kiss you? I am divorced, and even if I am to be a father, I have already made it clear that I will never be taking that woman back into my life."

"Well, yeah, but . . ."

"So unless you believe that kissing a single dad is somehow morally wrong, that first reason is no good," Bawaar said, shrugging and kissing her again.

Queenie blinked and looked up into his eyes. Who was this guy? Was he for real? Was he using her as a diversion from his family drama? Was he using her as a weapon to strike back against his psycho ex-wife? Did she even give a shit?

"There's like a hundred people standing outside that door," she whispered, feeling her resolve weaken to the point where it felt ridiculous to resist.

The Sheikh shrugged again. "And they were all inside the room when I kissed you the first time. I can invite them back in if you'd like."

He kissed her again as she giggled, and Queenie shook her head and touched his chest. God, he was big, she thought as she glanced down and gasped at the peaked front of his fitted trousers. He still had his tuxedo jacket on, but it was obscenely pushed out at the crotch, and Queenie instinctively reached down and undid the jacket, placing her hand on his hardness.

"Ya Allah," the Sheikh groaned, his right hand pulling on her hair, left hand circling around her and grabbing her ass.

What am I doing, Queenie wondered as she felt him close in for a ferocious kiss even as she tightened her fist around his tremendous cock. I can't do this! Who does this! What kind of woman am I?!

"Oh, God, I'm sorry," she gasped, letting go of his cock and pulling away from the kiss. "This is crazy. This is wrong. This is—"

She saw anger flash across the Sheikh's handsome face, and for a moment she wondered if he was going to throw her down on the carpet, rip her overalls down the seam, and take her face-down like an animal. But somehow he controlled himself, his jaw tightening into a forced smile as he shook his head and narrowed his eyes.

"All right then, go on," he said. "Leave. There is the door. Go on."

Queenie blinked as she held eye contact as long as she could. But then she looked away, turning her head toward the carpet near the mistletoe. She frowned as she saw the cluster of crumbs that she'd been called in to clean up in the first place, and then she glanced back at the Sheikh.

"Well," she said, "I'm still on the clock, and so I should probably finish the job before leaving."

The Sheikh followed her gaze and snorted when he saw the crumbs. "I agree. It is a mess down there, beneath the mistletoe. The crumbs are all the way in the carpet fibers. You might have to get down on your hands and knees to get all of them out."

Queenie nodded as she took two steps and then went down on her knees, leaning forward and raising her ass as she squinted at the few crumbs still left over from the Christmas cookie that had fallen from someone's plate.

"I might need some help here," she whispered.

"Of course," whispered the Sheikh from behind her, and Queenie felt her body stiffen when she realized he was down on his knees behind her. "I am known for being a hands-on boss. Here we go. Is that helping?"

Queenie gasped as she felt the Sheikh's large hands rest firmly on the rounds of her ass, caressing her gently and then squeezing hard. She arched her back down and moaned out loud, and the moment she felt his right hand slide between her thighs from behind she knew this was happening. She'd had her chance to walk away, and instead she'd gotten down on the floor like a whore and stuck her ass up like a goddamn slut.

Oh, God, Renita is right, Queenie thought as the Sheikh rubbed her mound roughly through her thick overalls, his face pushed up against her ass as she held firm. I am exactly what she called me! What the hell am I doing?! What the hell is *he* doing?! How is this ever gonna end well? In what world does the janitor ever end up with the freakin' CEO?

In no world outside of movies and romance novels, Queenie thought as she began to crawl away from the Sheikh, a chill running through her as she thought back to what she was running from . . . whom she was running from.

You need to run again, came the thought as she caught sight of her reflection in the floor-to-ceiling tinted windows that overlooked the dark parking lot. Run before you're trapped again. Before you're caught again. Before you have to run again. Run now, Queenie. Run, and keep running. You've screwed up again, and you need to run again. It's your own fault, you dumb slut. So get up and run.

She blinked in confusion as she felt the Sheikh reach beneath her and unzip the front of her blue overalls, shoving his hand inside her bra and groping her boobs, his fingers pinching her nipples as he continued to grind his face between her legs from behind. She could hear him grunt and growl behind her like an animal, but she knew she was the real beast here. She'd destroyed one marriage, ruined one family, and now she was on the verge of doing it again. Was it karma? Some messed up pattern that she was doomed to repeat? An attraction to the wrong kind of men?

Or do I turn good men into panting beasts when I get down on my knees and spread my fat ass like the filthy slut I am, Queenie wondered as her mother's words rang out like the crone was still alive, still in the damn room, watching, judging, pointing, laughing.

Through her tear-filled eyes Queenie saw red. She blinked and tried to focus. The Sheikh had pulled her overalls down past her shoulders, unclasped her bra from behind. She could hear him unbuckling and unzipping behind her, feel her own wetness flow into her panties. But she forced herself to focus on the red, and suddenly she realized the red was letters. Words. Two words.

Fire Exit.

Run, came the thought. Last chance to get out. Run.

And as her past reached out to her like fingers, claws, goddamn talons, Queenie kicked out with all she had, getting the Sheikh in the face with the heavy heel of her black, standard-issue utility boot. She heard him roar in pain, and then she was on her feet, her boobs hanging out, tears rolling down her cheeks as she raced for the exit like everything was on fire, like everything was in flames, like it was all burning down.

Again.

5
FIVE YEARS AGO
CHRISTMAS EVE
JUNO, ALASKA

"**I** ain't never seen so much smoke," said one of the onlookers.

"No smoke without a fire, like they say," replied someone else.

"Don't see any flames though," said a third person.

Queenie watched as the thick black smoke billowed out of the third-floor window. Her third floor window. The apartment building had apparently been cleared out in time, because the firefighters seemed fairly calm as they unwound their hoses and pointed their nozzles in the right direction. There was no one leaning out of windows screaming, "Help me!" There wasn't anyone on the street saying, "But my 100-pound Rottweiler is still in the apartment! Who's gonna save him?"

Who's gonna save *me*, Queenie wondered as she stared at the powerful stream of water blast in through her open third-floor window. I'm going down for this. Maybe prison for arson. Maybe bankruptcy court if they decide it was my fault and the insurance company refuses to pay.

But then Queenie had smiled, a strangely familiar calm washing over her when she reminded herself that they wouldn't find shit, that she'd done this before and gotten away with it, that she knew what she was doing. She didn't know *why* she did it, why she couldn't stop burning her way through life. But that was a problem to be solved some other day. For now, she could just bask in the warmth of another burning building.

She squinted as she tried to catch sight of the flames, but the folks in the crowd were right: You couldn't see any. Dammit, Queenie thought. She'd hoped to see the building light up like a goddamn Christmas tree! 'Twas the season, right?

"Merry Christmas to me," Queenie whispered as

she finally saw the orange tongues of flame lick their way around to the outside of the building. She smiled as the crowd oohed and aahed, the firemen began to move faster, the local TV cameras started to roll. "Merry Christmas to meee!!!"

6

"Merry Christmas to me," grunted the Sheikh as he examined his bleeding nose in the mirror of his private, executive restroom on the top floor of his now-empty office building. The party was over, the guests were gone, and his nose was swollen like Rudolph the damned Reindeer's.

He'd thought about sending his security personnel after that janitor, but he'd decided to let her go, let her run. He had enough drama in his life right then. He didn't need to add to it with some woman he barely knew, who clearly had her own issues.

Issues, yes, the Sheikh thought as he pushed a cotton swab up his nostril to soak up the blood. But ya

Allah, she also has curves. She also has spice. She also has goddamn *fire*!

And she makes me feel my own fire igniting, Bawaar thought as he pressed the ice-pack against the bridge of his nose, wondering if Queenie had broken it with her powerful kick. He grinned, immediately wincing in pain as he thought of her open overalls, the way her big nipples hardened when he pinched them, the way her feminine scent rose up to him when he pushed his hands down her panties and—

"Stop it," he said aloud, pain and arousal moving through him at the same time. He was hard beneath his trousers, erect in a way that he never remembered being with Renita. A flash of guilt passed across him, but he dismissed it and shook his head. No more guilt. He'd married Renita when he was too young and inexperienced to understand that some people were simply not compatible, simply not meant to be with each other. It was over, and that was for the best.

But she might be carrying my child, the Sheikh thought as he winced again. This time, however, it was not from physical pain but from the pain of imagining a future where Renita really was carrying the heir or heiress of Wakhrani! It would be a nightmare! He already knew she would never give up custody! After all, she came from a wealthy Jordanian family to begin with, and now after the divorce, her total assets would be well over one billion dollars! Even Renita was not greedy enough to give up custody for mere money. She wanted more. She wanted something else.

Bawaar stood and began to pace, like he always did when he was lost in thought. He glanced down at his bare feet, shaking his head and muttering as he pictured a timeline in his head. The last time he'd had sex with Renita was several months ago. Routine and unimaginative—in fact, if he remembered correctly, he'd closed his eyes and imagined someone else just to stay hard enough to get his release! That was when he'd known it was over, that this marriage would kill him if he did not get out. What sort of an omen was it if the heir of Wakhrani was conceived from such a lackluster union?

Again the Sheikh's mind was drawn to Queenie Quinn, the curvy janitor who'd teased him, toyed with him, and then kicked him in the face and run for the fire exit! Ya Allah, another madwoman in his life! Good riddance, yes?

Yes, the Sheikh thought. Put her out of your mind. You do not need any more drama. You do not need any more madness. You do not need . . .

Bawaar blinked as he saw that he was still hard, walking around barefoot and erect, his mind still full of images of a cleaning-lady's breasts, his senses still aroused by her lingering taste, her feminine scent!

This is what years of denying your primal needs has done to you, he reasoned. You never cheated on

Renita, but perhaps you should have! Perhaps you should have taken whores to bed when you felt dissatisfied with what your wife offered. Perhaps Renita would even have been relieved that you did not subject her to your animalistic needs that were clearly beyond her limits!

"But here we are," the Sheikh said out loud, tossing the ice-pack away and blowing his nose into a bloody silk handkerchief. "I am divorced, bleeding, and my balls are firmly in the cold hands of a woman I never want to see again."

Ya Allah, would it not be wonderful if Renita simply disappeared, the Sheikh thought. He caught sight of his reflection in the large window of his office as the dark fantasy passed through his mind, and he was startled by his own image: His face swollen and bruised; his cock still pushing against his trousers; blood stains on his white tuxedo shirt. He looked like a monster! Perhaps he was! Who else would even entertain the idea of getting rid of his ex-wife and their unborn child! And why? For that janitor?! Was he insane?! Was he still seriously thinking about Queenie Quinn when he had matters of monumental importance to work through?

His nose throbbed again as he allowed his thoughts to drift back to Queenie. There was no denying it. He wanted her. Perhaps it was because she'd turned him down, kicked him with a ferocity that he'd never seen in a woman. Perhaps he was just turned around from the drama Renita was throwing at him and he needed a release that was raw and primal, that gave life to his deepest urges, his darkest fantasies, needs that he'd suppressed so long as he'd tried to stay true in an unsatisfying marriage.

"But I am a king," he said out loud. "And I am now a single man. I will ignore Renita and focus on my own needs. And those needs come dressed in blue overalls and black utility boots, armed with a broom and dustpan, blessed with curves that remind me what it means to be a man."

The only question, the Sheikh thought as he felt Renita, the party, and everything else fade into the background while he allowed his mind to go where it wished, is whether she will show up to work again.

7

Do I even bother showing up at work again, Queenie thought as she stepped into the shower and stood there naked, shivering even though it was seventy degrees in her studio apartment and a balmy seventy-two outside. She wasn't sure if she felt guilty or violated, scared or angry, excited from running down the stairs and driving her beat-up Ford Escort at twenty-miles over the speed limit or still aroused from the way the Sheikh had touched her body, the way he'd prepared to take her . . . a way she knew she'd never been taken before.

"Tomorrow's Christmas Day, and it's a holiday," Queenie reasoned out loud as she let the warm water blast against her naked curves. "So I've got a day to decide."

And so does he, she thought as she soaped herself, feeling a tingle as she touched her crotch and realized her pubic hair was matted and sticky from how wet she'd gotten, how wet she still was. He's got a day to think about whether or not he wants to press charges for being kicked in the face!

Oh, God, what do I do if the cops show up at my door with handcuffs and a warrant?! I can't afford a lawyer! And some overworked public defender isn't going to match up with some billionaire's team of lawyers! What happens if he threatens to sue me unless I . . .

Queenie couldn't complete the thought because her mind began to spin, her body began to shake, her lips began to tremble. She couldn't deny that the thought scared her to some degree. But it also turned her on in a sick, twisted way. Blackmailed into screwing your boss? Sucking his thick cock beneath the table? Bending over and letting him take you any way he wanted, any*where* he wanted?! Oh, shit, now *that* was something straight from the pages of the books she'd obsessively read as a young teenager up in Juno, the stuff that had kept her young body warm on those cold Alaskan nights.

Queenie closed her eyes as she thought back to the night her mother had walked into her room and seen thirteen-year-old Queenie with her nightie pulled up over her boobs, her legs spread wide, one hand inside her panties, the other furiously reading through a novel with some bare-chested beast of a man on the cover.

"My daughter is a whore," Mama had said at the breakfast table the next morning. "A young harlot in the making. It's unnatural at such an early age, Queenie. You shouldn't be having these feelings. And you damned well shouldn't be touching yourself like that! Have you no shame? Do you even understand how disgusting you are? I don't know if I can even *look* at you again after seeing you like that! My own daughter! I wouldn't even believe it if you hadn't come out of me!"

Queenie had cried all the way through breakfast, barely eating for like the first time ever. The look on her mother's face when she'd opened the door the previous night was burned in little Queenie's memory, and even now, two decades later, it brought tears to Queenie's eyes. She knew, of course, that it was perfectly normal for a teenage girl to fantasize about being taken by a man, but the emotional imprint of that incident was too deep to be erased. And when Queenie began dating, discovering to her delight that having big boobs as a fourteen-year-old made her very much in demand despite her fat ass and double-chin, her reaction to being touched seemed to back up her mother's accusation that Queenie was just a harlot in training.

And so Queenie decided to accept it. To embrace it. To just shrug and say sure, all right, let's do it. You wanna suck my boobs beneath the bleachers? Sure! You wanna finger my pussy in the detention room after school? Great! You wanna jerk off all over my ass in the backseat of your mom's minivan? Have at it! That's who I am. That's what Mama said I am.

She'd taken on all comers through her teenage years, and soon enough everyone was saying exactly what Queenie's mama had told her when she was thirteen: You want an easy lay? Call Queenie! She'll do it with ya!

It had all been fun and games until Queenie began to hear the rumors, what boys and girls and even the teachers were saying about her. And then the School Counselor had called Queenie into her office and spoken to her about things like reputation, safety, hygiene . . . basically saying Queenie was a filthy, dirty, slut. At least that was the way Queenie heard it, and then everything was backing up what Mama had said to her at the breakfast table all those years ago! Mama was right! Queenie was growing up to be a dirty girl, a filthy slut, a wanton whore!

And so Queenie just shut down. She shut it all down. Don't touch me. Don't call me. Don't fucking talk to me. She'd withdrawn from the world her senior year in high school, crying in relief when the year ended and she didn't have to face all those kids again, face her own guilt and shame when she saw how the boys she'd fucked and sucked would look at her in class, wink at her when no one was looking, whisper things when no one else was listening. It took her to the brink of despair several times, the edge of wanting to do something drastic, to somehow make up for her sins, to cleanse herself of the filth everyone said was inside her.

And then she'd discovered fire. The ultimate cleanser. A way to erase the past, present, and future all at once.

She'd started by burning all her clothes, every top that had ever been unbuttoned by a boy, every skirt and dress that had ever been pushed up, every pair of panties, all her bras. She'd watched them burn in a little pile in the clearing behind her house when Mama wasn't home, and it had given her a sense of peace, relief, pure calm. It was addictive, and Queenie found herself slowly opening up to life again now that she'd found this private way to cleanse herself.

Of course, Mama wasn't happy to learn that Queenie suddenly needed a whole set of new clothes.

"What happened to all the lovely dresses I bought you last year?" Mama had asked. "And why do you need new underwear? Don't tell me the old ones don't fit anymore! Queenie!"

"Never mind," Queenie had said. "I'll buy them myself. I'll get a job and pay for them myself."

And so within a week of graduating high school, Queenie was working full-time at a gas-station on the outskirts of Juno. It was on the bus route, and so she didn't need a car. It paid well enough, and Queenie liked talking to customers as she rang them up at the register. She even liked going outside in the cold when someone pulled up at the Full Service pump and honked their horn.

There was one green car that pulled into the Full Service spot every few days, always around the time when the Full Service attendant would go on break and Queenie was in charge of everything. She didn't notice the driver the first few times—he always went into the station to use the restroom while she filled the tank. He'd swipe his credit card at the pump, adjust his hat and sunglasses, and then drive off without ever tipping her.

Then one day he started tipping her. A twenty dollar bill the first day. Forty the next. A crisp hundred the week after that.

"Um, Sir, this is a hundred!" Queenie had said, blinking as she tried to see the man's eyes through his mirrored sunglasses.

"I know!" he'd said, finally taking off those glasses and smiling in a way that made Queenie's heart jump. He was a bit older, but handsome, with clear blue eyes and an easy smile. She'd seen something in his eyes, something that made her want to know more about him. "I won the lottery! Gonna get a new car tomorrow!" He'd paused, rubbing his fresh-shaved chin. "You want this one?"

Queenie's eyes had gone wide as she looked at the green Chevy. It was old, but she knew it was in good condition. The engine hummed quietly, and there were no dents or dings she could see. She'd peeked inside several times while pumping gas, and it always looked clean and organized. No fast-food bags or candy wrappers. No stains on the seats. Yeah, it looked clean, just like the man did. Clean and organized. Queenie had never been around "clean and organized"! It was just Mama and Queenie at home, and neither of them were particularly neat or organized.

"Um, what do you mean?" Queenie asked, blinking as she looked into the man's blue eyes and then at the car again. The hundred-dollar bill felt cool in her hand, and she closed her fist over it as she looked back at the man. Then she shook her head as she thought about what Mama would say if she came home with a car and a hundred bucks—both given to her by a blue-eyed stranger!

"I mean it's yours. Take it. Here," the man said, leaning in through the open driver's side window and pulling the keys out. There were a lot of keys on the ring, and the man got the big car key off and handed it to her. "There you go." He blinked once, as if something had just occurred to him. "Oh, I'll need your full name and address."

"What?" Queenie had said, frowning as a chill came over her. This sounded like the kinda thing kids were warned about, right? Handsome stranger offering you candy . . . or a car!

"So I can sign the car over to you," the man said, breaking into a warm smile that put Queenie at ease. "That way, if you do something horrible with the car, they won't come knocking on my door!"

Queenie had laughed, touching her hair as the man smiled and took a step closer. He told her about winning the lottery: It wasn't millions, but it sounded like it was a hell of a lot—especially for Juno. Once again he held that key out, and once again Queenie hesitated. A hundred-dollar bill was one thing, but a car? Seriously?! For free? Nothing was for free! He'd want something in return, right? Sooner or later he'd want what all those boys wanted.

She'd frowned as she looked back into his eyes. So what, she'd thought. He's attractive. I don't see a wedding ring. Yeah, it's weird that he wants to give me stuff, but didn't a lot of romance novels start off with a rich, socially-awkward man showering a woman with expensive gifts because he wants her—wants *all* of her, not just her body?

Maybe this is my love story, Queenie had thought,

blinking and then slowly taking the key, shivering as his fingers touched her wrist. Maybe Mama was wrong. Maybe I'm not meant to be a whore but a lady, a sophisticated woman who drives around in a clean car, wears sunglasses and lipstick, goes to fancy restaurants with a blue-eyed man of wealth and stature! Why not? Maybe I've burned away my past, and this is my future right here, staring me in the face, touching my hand, giving me a car!

"Queenie Quinn," the man said, glancing down as Queenie wrote out her name and address in the small notebook he'd handed her. "How old are you, Queenie?"

"Nineteen," Queenie had said, touching her hair again and standing as straight as she could. "How about you?"

The man had laughed, shaking his head and winking. "Not so old that I don't remember being nineteen," he said. "You have a drivers license, Queenie?"

Queenie shook her head, her face going red when she remembered she'd failed her driving test at sixteen and never retaken it. It hadn't seemed like a priority at the time, since even Mama didn't own a car and no way in hell was Queenie gonna be able to afford one anytime soon.

The man raised an eyebrow. "Wait, do you even know how to drive?" he asked.

Queenie shrugged, a half-smile emerging as she

shook her head and narrowed her brown eyes at him. "How hard can it be?" she said.

The man broke into laughter, shaking his head and touching her on the arm. "You are priceless! So you were going to take my car and then just . . . figure out how to drive it?!"

Queenie blinked and nodded. "I guess."

"All right," the man said, snorting once and shaking his head. "What time you get off work?"

"Midnight."

"OK. I'll meet you here at midnight. For your first driving lesson. Once I'm convinced you aren't a danger to yourself or anyone else, the car is yours. Deal?"

Queenie had smiled, looking into his blue eyes and willing herself to trust him, to trust that this was the beginning of her very own love story. "Sure," she'd said. "It's a deal."

He'd made good on the deal after five lessons. Five lessons during which they talked and smiled, flirted and laughed, hands touching as he showed her the gear shift, bodies brushing against one another as she got in and out of the driver's seat.

Then, on the fifth day, he leaned over and kissed her. She'd kissed him back, and they made love in the backseat of that clean green Chevy. He was gentle and careful, and Queenie drove home alone feeling like she was glowing, like she was a woman, like her past didn't matter because her future was here, her happily-ever-after had arrived! Who said she was destined to be a whore?! To hell with you, Mama!

But then, two months later, hell arrived at Queenie's doorstep in the form of a woman with two children in tow.

"Your daughter is a whore!" the woman was screaming when Queenie made it out of her room to see what the commotion was about. "You tell her to find her own man, because this one is taken! You should be ashamed! Both of you should be ashamed! She seduces a married man, gets him to give her cash and even our car! Where is she?! Where's that slut? Where is she? I want her to see the family she's ruined. I want her to look my children in the eye and explain to them why their daddy just filed for divorce!"

Queenie burned that green car later that night. She drove it out past city limits, stuffed a rag and some cotton balls into the gas tank, and then watched it burst into beautiful flames as she sat on her haunches and cried. Then after the flames died down she laughed, realizing she now needed to walk like three miles before she could get to a bus-stop.

Mama barely spoke to her again after that. The next time she even brought up the topic was when Mama mentioned that the blue-eyed man had stopped by to see her.

"Wait, what?" Queenie had said. "When?"

"A couple days ago. I told him you were gone," Mama had replied, barely looking up from doing her nails.

"Gone? I'm right here!"

Mama had looked up then, her face more wrinkled than ever, like she'd aged ten years over the past few months. "When will you learn, Queenie? When will you learn not to make the mistakes I did?"

Queenie had frowned as she wondered what the hell Mama meant. Then she got it. "My father? He was married?"

Mama slowly nodded, focusing on her nails again even though her hands were shaking. "Married. Two kids. House in Anchorage." She smiled and shook her head. "He said his marriage was over, that he was leaving her, that we'd be a family. He never even set eyes upon you, Queenie."

Queenie closed her eyes and moved close to her mother. She took the woman's hands in hers, squeezed gently and smiled. Then she picked up the bottle of nail polish, smiled again, and finished doing Mama's nails in silence.

"So I was a mistake?" Queenie said softly, just as she got to Mama's left pinky.

Mama had taken a breath, pulling her hand away and reaching for Queenie's face. She'd cupped Queenie's face in her hands and looked her dead on. "Yes, but you were the only mistake I *don't* regret."

Queenie had cried, and they'd hugged, Mama's blue nail polish getting all over Queenie's red sweater. She thought to ask about her father, find out his name, where he lived. But then she'd held back, a part of her not wanting to know. Never wanting to know. Why should she give a damn about a man who didn't give a damn about her, who'd never even bothered to look upon his daughter's face, who'd lied and cheated and then turned his back on Mama?

"Did he even pay child support?" Queenie asked. "He must have paid child support. Or else he'd be in jail right now."

Mama had shrugged. "Maybe he is," she said with a snort. Then she shook her head. "I didn't want a cent of that man's money. You were mine, and mine alone. My angel. My pearl. The diamond of my life."

Queenie had swallowed hard as she looked into her mother's eyes that day. A part of her respected the pride that burned fiercely in the woman. But another part of her wanted to smack Mama upside the head and point to the peeling paint in their crappy home, the pile of unpaid bills, the stress they'd both gone through over the years. And all for what?! Pride?! Self-respect?! You shoulda sued his sorry ass for everything he had, Queenie wanted to scream. You owed me that! Maybe I wouldn't have had to postpone college to work at a gas-station! Maybe I would've grown up with more self-respect of my own! You traded your own sense of self-worth for mine, you selfish bitch!

The thoughts had come out of nowhere, carrying a rage with them that made Queenie's hands shake as she forced a smile and said she had to go to the bathroom. She'd stood there in the bathroom, staring at the dripping faucet, pulling out the book of matches that she carried with her like a smoker carried a pack of Marlboros. She absentmindedly began lighting the matches one by one, tossing them into the toilet and smiling at the way they sizzled and died. She thought of her blue-eyed lover, a dark feeling of perverse satisfaction coming over her when she decided that hell, he *was* leaving his wife for her, wasn't he? And Queenie wasn't even pregnant or anything! He wanted Queenie! What was wrong with that? Didn't a man have the right to choose his mate? How was it Queenie's business if he'd chosen to leave his wife and kids? People made mistakes. Maybe the wife was a soul-sucking shrew! Maybe the kids were annoying little brats! Maybe her blue-eyed lover was sitting alone in a motel room pining away for her! Whose business was it? Not Mama's! Not anyone else's! It was just him and her, wasn't it?

Queenie had stared at herself in the mirror, a pout making her cheeks look big and round as she began to strike two matches at once, furiously tossing them at the toilet as she ripped through the book. She closed her eyes as she inhaled the pungent scent of sulphur and flame, and it was only when she smelled smoke that she opened her eyes again and gasped in shock.

"Oh, *shit!*" she screamed, realizing that she'd missed the toilet with the last few matches and now the stack of toilet-paper rolls were a ball of flame! She grabbed a towel and tried to smother the flames, but the towel was a cheap cotton blend that simply caught fire too!

Queenie had stared as the nylon shower curtain got in on the fun, and it was only when she felt the heat on her face that she realized it was time to get out. She looked at the beautiful flames one more time, and then she turned and headed for Mama.

"Mama, where are you?" she'd screamed when she got to the living room and saw nothing but the bottles of nail polish. "*Mama!*"

Queenie had run to the front door and pulled it open, hoping that Mama had already made her way outside. But there was no one there. Then she turned and glanced at the stairs, a chill coming over her when she realized Mama must have gone upstairs to use the other bathroom!

The flames were already licking their way out past the main-floor bathroom, swallowing up the dry particle-board that pretended to be walls in their shitty little home. She glanced at the phone, knowing she should be calling 911. But the flames would be at the stairs soon, and so Queenie decided that the neighbors would have to call 911 because she needed to get upstairs and get Mama out of there!

But when she got to the second floor, Queenie saw to her dismay that the bathroom door was wide open and there was no one inside! And that's when it hit her: Mama had been doing laundry earlier, and she must have headed to the basement to move the clothes to the dryer!

Queenie almost went down the stairs head first, somehow keeping her balance as she got to the basement stairs. She heard her mother scream, and she screamed back as she saw thick black smoke flowing from down below. The fire must have already burned through the thin floor of the bathroom, which meant the basement ceiling was about to collapse!

She coughed as she closed her eyes to the smoke and felt her way down the stairs. The guilt of what she'd done was making her choke worse than the smoke, and Queenie was sobbing when she finally got to Mama and grabbed the woman by the arms, pulling her back up the stairs as fast as she could.

They got out the front door just as the fire trucks pulled up, and Queenie lay back and pulled Mama close as the flames waved at them as if to say goodbye, like something had ended.

And something had ended, because Mama died three days later, alone in a hospital, of an undiagnosed brain aneurysm. Completely unrelated to the smoke inhalation, the doctors had assured Queenie when she arrived at the hospital after getting the call at work. It would have happened anyway.

"Woulda happened anyway," Queenie said out loud as she pushed away the memory and tried to focus on the matter at hand. Wasn't "woulda happened anyway" just another term for destiny? Fate? Meant to be? Was there ever gonna be a "meant to be" for her? Was she ever going to be able to get past the guilt, the shame, the shadow of being a mistake, a disappointment, a home-wrecker, a whore, slut, and everything else she'd been called in her life? What was next? Burn this life and keep running? Or make your stand here?

She glanced at her janitor's overalls sitting neatly folded on the chair beside her bed. She'd been given two sets when she started work at the Wakhrani Group, and when she saw the crumpled set on the floor next to the chair, Queenie sensed that it represented a choice. The choice to face the patterns of her life and take control of them, or burn it all down and run away again. Stay and fight, or turn and hide.

"No more hiding," she whispered to herself as she reached for the clean set of overalls. "If this is who you are, it's time to embrace it. If your destiny is to always be attracted to the wrong sort of men, then maybe you just need to face that truth and embrace it. Make your stand here, Queenie. You thought you had a blue-eyed prince once and he turned out to be a frog. Now you've got a green-eyed king standing before you, so what're you gonna do about it?"

Queenie and the king, she thought with a smile, nodding as she felt her resolve strengthen, her confidence soar. Maybe that *is* my destiny. I'm not settling for some prince. I'm gonna get a goddamn *king*! After all, Mama named me Queenie, not Princess.

8
CHRISTMAS DAY

It might not be so bad to have a Prince or Princess playing in these empty hallways, Sheikh Bawaar thought as he made his way down the wide sandstone passage toward the West Atrium of Wakhrani's Royal Palace. *Just so long as it is not from that woman's womb.*

"When did these arrive?" the Sheikh barked at the attendant who'd handed him the manila folder with test results apparently validating Renita's claim that she was carrying his child. Of course, Renita had the ways and means to produce a report that verified she was carrying the lovechild of Hitler and JFK if she wanted, so the results alone were meaningless without the Sheikh's own tests—meaningless to him, at least. Perhaps they might create some problems in a courtroom. Certainly they would create waves in the press.

Renita had been oddly silent after that outburst at the Christmas party—though the Sheikh had left the United States directly after the party, with no intention of returning until the New Year. He'd given the company the entire week off, which had always been the plan. Good plan, he told himself as he dismissed his attendant and strolled out toward the open atrium, along cobbled sandstone pathways studded with emeralds and rubies, fountains made of polished black Italian marble, teakwood gazebos hand-crafted by artisans from a century ago. He sighed as once again he pictured children running along the pathways, playing in the fountains, carving their names into the old wood of the gazebos. He'd been an only child, even though his father had taken four wives. Certainly he would have been one of many children if his father had lived long enough—the little he remembered of the man made Bawaar think fatherhood was something the old Sheikh took very seriously.

"You will be the old Sheikh soon," Bawaar said, leaning over the edge of a lotus pool and staring at his reflection in the still water. "And Father did not live long enough to deserve the title of Old Sheikh! Ya Allah, he barely lived long enough to deserve the title of Father!"

Indeed, the "old Sheikh" had died before he was thirty, leaving behind four wives and one infant son. An heir. A prince. The boy with the sole responsibility of carrying on the Royal Line of Wakhrani—a responsibility his four mothers had never let him forget.

They'd arranged the marriage with Renita when Bawaar turned eighteen. By then he'd already been Sheikh for two years—officially, at least. Unofficially he'd been sitting on the throne since he was old enough to climb up there! He'd always loved the throne, loved everything about being Sheikh. He could not wait to impart everything he'd learned to a son or daughter, whoever would sit on the throne after he moved on to the next world.

"Stop with this melancholy and reflection," Bawaar said, chuckling when he realized he was reflecting while staring at his . . . reflection. "Remember who you are. You are a man. A king. You create your own destiny, take what you want from life, make no apologies, leave no prisoners! You were raised by four women. You got married when you were eighteen. Your entire life you have been controlled by women, and now, when you finally declare your freedom, cast off the shackles Renita slipped around you during those dark years of unfulfillment, you are once again allowing yourself to fall under the control of women!"

The Sheikh spat into the lotus pool, straightening up to full height as the image of Queenie Quinn played at the corners of his mind. He'd thought about her for ten hours straight on his private jet, sipping tea and staring out the window. He'd imagined her curves as he gazed at the swell of the sand dunes on the ride back to the Palace. He'd remembered how she tasted, how she smelled, how she felt up against him as he bathed in the solitude of his private chambers. Was all of that just his mind looking for an escape, searching for the furthest thing from Renita? Or was there something more here?

Ya Allah, the Sheikh thought as he rubbed his stubble. I truly do not know! I was married when I was eighteen! Renita was the first and only woman I ever touched! I never went away to college! I never had harems or whores or high-school crushes! My mothers were even careful about the attendants they assigned to my private chambers, lest I be tempted by some commoner! By God, they did a number on me, did they not?! In a way I have been dormant all my life, my true self never really waking up, the sexual animal inside me never truly getting a chance to stretch its muscles!

So perhaps what I felt with this American woman is not just a release but an awakening, the Sheikh thought as he ran his fingers through his hair and then glanced at his diamond-studded Rolex. It was early in the afternoon in Wakhrani, which meant it was still Christmas morning back in the United States. Children all over America would be waking up to see what Santa had brought them. Did the Sheikh not deserve a Christmas gift as well? Perhaps a woman that he actually *wanted*? Maybe a child created by two people making wild, free love?

The pieces came together in Bawaar's mind so fast he almost shouted out loud. Yes! Of course! Why in Allah's name not?! He was a king, goddamn it! His mothers were no more. His wife had proved herself to be a madwoman. It was time for him to take control of his life, of himself, of his damned needs!

And right now he had just one need.

So he picked up his private line and dialed, glancing at his watch again and smiling when he realized that if they timed it right, he would have his Christmas present delivered before the clock ticked past midnight in Wakhrani.

9

It was seven in the morning, and Queenie was still wide awake. She hadn't slept a wink, and her eyes were burning because she'd barely even blinked, her thoughts were so wild and convoluted. She'd gone back over her entire life, at one point rummaging through the kitchen drawers to find a book of matches. She just wanted to light one and see the flame. But she'd kept the apartment clear of matches and lighters, and although she could have lit the electric stove and set some paper on fire, she'd managed to resist the urge. This was an apartment building with families and kids. She wasn't a goddamn psycho. She just hated herself, not everyone else!

"Merry Christmas to me," she whispered as she

walked out of the bedroom alcove and stared at the box containing the artificial tree she'd ordered online. The box hadn't even been opened. She'd barely had time after starting this new job, which was perhaps the most physically demanding thing she'd done in a while. Who knew vacuuming carpets and taking out the trash burned so much energy?

"Well, there's also being groped by your billionaire boss, breaking his nose, and then running for the goddamn fire exit," Queenie muttered as she wondered if she'd imagined all of it, if Christmas Eve had never happened. Then she wondered if she could change her past simply by wishing hard enough. In her sleepless, manic state it seemed almost plausible! Close your eyes and imagine what you want, Queenie! What do you want for Christmas?

She got down on her knees and began to open that box with the Christmas tree. The tree was small enough that it came in one piece, and she stood it up, folded down the wire-branches, and gazed at the green plastic needles. She had no ornaments to hang on the bare branches, but that seemed strangely appropriate, given the emptiness of her life.

"What do you want your life to be filled with, Queenie?" she said out loud, closing her eyes as she leaned forward on her knees and held on to the tree like it was a magical artifact that would grant her Christmas wish. "What do you want?"

She felt a slight breeze around her bare ankles as

she let her thoughts flow free, let them take form on their own, let her instincts answer the question of what she wanted for Christmas. Again her life flashed past her eyes like the Ghost of Christmas Past: All the mistakes she'd made, how she herself was a mistake, an accidental pregnancy, unplanned, unscheduled, unwanted . . .

"I want to be wanted," she whispered as that breeze got steadier. "And I want a child that feels wanted, that *is* wanted! That's what I want for Christmas. Yup. Whoever's listening, that's what I want for Christmas."

She frowned as she finally realized that the breeze wasn't her imagination. She turned and saw that the window near the fire escape was somehow wide open even though she always kept it shut.

"Santa?" she said out loud, trying to smile even though she felt a strange chill go through her. "Sorry, I didn't set out any cookies and milk for you. Hopefully that won't get me on the naughty list."

Santa didn't answer, but Queenie heard a sound from behind her that was too loud to be a mouse stirring. She turned slowly as that chill rose up her spine, the blood pounded in her ears, her vision blurred. Then she stared at the three masked men standing before her, and just as one of them stepped forward with a handkerchief that smelled like chemicals, she smiled and nodded, deciding that these were the ghosts of Christmas Past, Present, and Future.

10

"The past does not matter. The future is too far away to be relevant. And the present is . . . you. You are my present. My gift. My Christmas miracle," came the Sheikh's unmistakable voice through Queenie's chemical hallucination. "How do you feel?"

Queenie groaned and blinked, rubbing her neck as she tried to focus. "Like I've been wrapped in a stocking for a week. How're you?"

The Sheikh laughed, clapping his hands once, the sound making Queenie wince.

"OK, can we keep the noise level down, please?" she said. "I'm having a very nice hallucination, and I don't want to be interrupted before I ask the Ghost of Christmas Future some questions."

"Ya Allah," the Sheikh said, completely ignoring her request and clapping three more times like this was a circus and she was the performer. "Excellent! You have just been drugged, kidnapped, and transported halfway across the world, and yet you are calm and focused."

Queenie blinked. "Calm? More like still drugged. As for focused . . . well, I can see you clearly enough, if that counts. Oh, wait, I actually *can't* see you clearly. Scratch that." She blinked again, gazing up at the high, domed ceilings of the room she was in. "Where am I?" she said, frowning. "Why is this room so big?"

"It is not a room, it is the Eastern day-chambers of Wakhrani's Royal Palace. It is bathed in sunlight from seven in the morning until three in the afternoon, and for over a century my ancestors have been using it to conduct business, pleasure, and everything in between."

Queenie looked around as the Sheikh stood and spread his arms out wide. He wore black silk pajamas—not the kind you sleep in—and a red robe that was more cloak than robe, now that Queenie thought about it. And why was she thinking about what he was wearing, anyway, she wondered as her frown deepened. She glanced to her left, and only then did she notice that what she thought was a black wall was in fact a massive open balcony facing the dark expanse of night. Slowly she made out stars . . . one, two, then a hundred, now a thousand of them! It looked like a million diamonds set in black velvet, and she gasped and stood up, feeling the need to look out into that darkness.

But her legs were wobbly from being drugged, and about a second after she managed to stand up, her knees buckled and she crumpled to the floor, her mouth hanging open as she watched the intricately designed carpet come rushing up to meet her.

She didn't fall onto the carpet—though it seemed plush enough to cushion her fall. Instead she felt an incredibly strong arm slip around her waist, a hard body press against hers as the Sheikh swooped in and caught her as she fell.

"Ya Allah," he muttered. "Those imbeciles gave you a double dose. I would have them beheaded for this, but it is my fault for not sending my most trusted men. I had no choice, though. I had to go with men who were already in the United States. Time was of the essence."

"Why?" Queenie said, leaning against his hard body like it was a perfectly reasonable thing to do. "Why are we in your day-chambers when it's night outside? What kind of stupidity is that?"

The Sheikh laughed in surprise. "That is what is most confusing to you in all this? Not the fact that I have kidnapped you and brought you to my palace?"

Queenie pushed against his chest, her breath catching when her palms rested against his massive pectorals. God, he was muscular. Big and hard, tall and straight. So handsome. Such smooth, clear brown skin. And those eyes!

Queenie blinked as she felt her senses return in a rush, and now the panic came riding in like a stampede of horses. Her breathing quickened, her heart raced, and the blood pounded in her temples as she blinked several times and fought back the shock.

"The last thing I remember was being in my apartment and wishing . . . wishing for . . ." she gasped, looking up into his green eyes and then away from him, blinking again. Was this real? It felt real. *He* felt real. It had to be real. She didn't drink or do drugs. She didn't believe in ghosts, alternate realities, or honest-to-God miracles. So this was real, which meant it was . . . insane. Straight-up insane!

She felt her vision contract, and at first she thought she might pass out. But then Queenie just started to giggle. Perhaps it was the drug, but she didn't feel drunk or stoned or intoxicated. She clearly remembered what she'd been thinking about before she'd been taken: She'd been thinking about the Sheikh. Thinking that she wanted him, that he was gonna be her king, her happily ever after, just like in those books she'd read obsessively while alone in her room, one hand absentmindedly shoved down the front of her worn-out cotton panties.

She giggled again as she thought about some of

those stories where some rich guy or ruthless criminal (always with six-pack abs and a chiseled chin—whatever that meant) kidnapped a woman because he liked how her ass looked in harem pants or a Victorian gown or whatever the time-period and setting required. The woman would either scream her head off or just gasp and faint, either break down like a little girl or get "feisty" with the hero, threaten to sue him, kill him, or just kick him in the balls. But then the hero would take what he wanted, show her that his cock was the solution to all her problems (and his too . . .), she would get knocked up against her will, escape from captivity or reject him outright, only to return with triplets in her arms and love in her heart. The end.

But I don't wanna fight him off, Queenie thought as she glanced at the twinkling stars over the desert sky. And I'm not going to faint, scream, or throw a tantrum. I wanted this. I chose this. I asked for this.

And I'm accepting it. I'm accepting my Christmas Miracle. I'm taking my king. No more drama. No push and pull. No whimpering and saying, "Unhand me, you brute!" In fact I *want* his hands back on me, and I'm not ashamed to say it. In my story, the heroine *is* asking for it! Fuck it. This is the new romance, a happily-ever-after for today's woman. You got some crazy ex-wife who says she's got your kid? Big deal. I'll one-up her. Show her I'm in it to win it.

"In it to win it," she whispered as clarity returned to her body and mind at the same time. Her mother was dead. Her past was burned down and buried in the Alaskan snow. It was time to embrace who she was. Slut? Whore? Harlot? All right. So what? You jealous that I've got the self-confidence to just shrug and go for what I want without any more shame, any more guilt, any more hypocritical bitches pointing their self-righteous fingers at me and calling me names for doing something they *wish* they got a chance to do?

"What did you say?" came the Sheikh's voice through her daydream—or nightdream, really. Waking dream. Whatever. "You are mumbling."

"Then you'd better shut me up with a kiss," she replied firmly, looking up into his eyes as she felt the wetness ooze into her panties. Then she glanced past him, checking the time on a massive grandfather clock encased in hand-carved teakwood, decorated with intricate Arabic inscriptions, the hands made of a metal that looked like gold . . . probably because it *was* gold. "And since it's still Christmas for another hour or so, why don't you finish this Christmas story and knock me up while you're at it. Let's get this Christmas Miracle signed and sealed. Get this gift wrapped. Put a bow on it. Get it tied and—"

And then she couldn't speak, because the Sheikh had indeed shut her up with a kiss, a kiss that exploded her world, erased the past, made the present and the future roll into one and then disappear into the diamond-studded Arabian night until there was nothing left but him and her, a man and a woman, Queenie and her King.

11

Of course that is the answer, the Sheikh thought as he dug his fingers into her hair, slid his other hand down the back of her panties, pushed his tongue deep into her mouth as he kissed her with a desperation he'd never felt. *She* is the answer! The complete opposite of everything I hated in Renita. She brings to me everything that Renita drained from me. This woman adds to my power, reminds me that I am a man and that she is a woman, that I am a king and she is my queen.

And of course a queen will feel no shame to ask for what she wants, to *demand* what she wants!

Ya Allah, Bawaar thought as he felt her hands claw

at his cock through his silk pajamas, her touch almost making him explode right then and there. What this queen wants is a child. A child conceived on Christmas Day! She has decided to step into the ring with Renita, to beat that woman at her own game! No shame. No hesitation. The confidence of a queen who knows what she wants and is not ashamed to spread her legs to get it!

The Sheikh felt his mouth widen in a grin as he pulled her top off and buried his face between her breasts, the fingers of his left hand firmly wedged in her rear crack, his right hand deftly snapping off her bra from behind.

Her magnificent breasts popped into full view as Queenie's bra fell off, and the Sheikh groaned out loud and then took her right nipple into his mouth, sucking so hard she screamed and arched her back. Her fingers were buried deep in his thick hair, and he could feel the pain in his scalp as she clawed and pulled at his locks. He moved to her other nipple, biting gently but firmly as he drove his middle finger into her asshole, bringing forth another scream of surprised pleasure from his queen, his Queenie.

"Ya Allah, I have never been so aroused," he growled, pulling back from her breasts and looked down past their bodies at the way she was firmly pulling on his cock through his pajamas. He groaned again, feeling his balls tighten already as if they were preparing for the biggest orgasm of his life. But at the same time he knew he would not come until he was inside her. His body would not allow it. Although there was no way either of them could know for sure, somehow the Sheikh knew he was going to impregnate her tonight, on the first damned try. He was going to do it, by Allah. Give her what she wanted. Commit to her right now, in the flesh, with his seed.

He pulled her hand away from his cock, moving down along her body and yanking off her unbuttoned jeans. Her panties were a crumbled, wet mess, and he gasped at the sight of the dark patch at the soaked crotch, his mouth salivating as her scent came up to him and drew him close like a magnet. One deep breath and then his face was jammed in there, his tongue pushing the damp cotton up between the dark lips of her slit. He could taste her, and he swallowed like he needed to possess her nectar, own her essence, like it gave him strength the way a magic potion gave the gods of myth special powers.

"Please, Bawaar," she groaned, spreading her thighs all the way wide as the Sheikh began to lick the insides of her loins like an animal. "Please fuck me. Fuck me now."

Her words almost made him blow his load, but his balls seized up tight like they were reminding him that he was in control of his body and of hers as well. He would fuck her, and by Allah he would fuck her hard, pouring every last drop of his thick semen into her. But not yet. Not until he decided. She was his queen, but he was the king. And she needed to know that he was the king. Now and forever.

"I will fuck you when I am ready," he growled, pulling down her panties and tossing them away. He held her thighs down and apart, breathing deep of her feminine musk as he stared directly at her glistening red slit open wide for him, her matted brown curls neatly arranged around it like it had been designed by divine hands. "First you will come for me. At my command. Yes?"

"Yes," she whispered, bucking her hips up toward his face and arching her neck back. "So long as you give the command pretty damned soon."

The Sheikh smiled and shook his head. "Not yet," he whispered, lowering his mouth to her open slit and then gently blowing on her. She moaned and shuddered as he blew warm air against her stiff little clit, making her hairs flutter like desert grass as she began to writhe and thrash under his strong grip. "Not until I allow it."

"What are you doing to me?" she groaned. "Oh, God, I don't think I can hold it."

"You can and you will. I am your king, and I am also your boss, by the way. So you will not come until I allow it."

Queenie gasped, her eyes rolling back in her head,

her mouth contorting as she squirmed under the Sheikh's hold. Then she opened her eyes and blinked as if she was trying to focus. "I don't think denying me the right to have an orgasm is covered in the employee handbook. And if it is, it's most certainly . . . oh, oh, *God!*"

The Sheikh stared in wonder as Queenie came, her orgasm clearly whipping through her body like a wave. Bawaar swore he could see it move through her like something real and tangible, and the sight of her losing her mind from arousal almost made him come too.

And then suddenly he was inside her, all of it happening so fast he could barely remember what had happened. He had slipped off his pajamas, positioned his cockhead to her open slit, and driven all the way in with one hard stroke, flexing inside her once and then immediately beginning to pump as she screamed and came harder.

"Oh, *fuck!*" she howled as he contracted his muscular ass and rammed himself into her again, the sensation of her warm depths around his swollen cock so divine that the Sheikh almost wept.

So many years I tortured myself by staying loyal to that woman when someone like this was out there waiting for me, he thought. Just for me. For me alone.

There was no doubt in Bawaar's mind as he pulled back and pushed himself into her again, smiling as he saw beads of perspiration appear on her forehead like droplets of dew on a flower. No doubt that she was his, that he was claiming her as his . . . his everything. Lover, mistress, whore, wife, queen, employee . . . whatever. It did not matter what label they put on it, because no word could come close to describing how sublime it was to feel her from the inside like this.

"Ya Allah," he whispered as his orgasm rolled in silently at first, his balls seizing up as his peak approached. Then it hit him, and his balls released their load through his strained cock as the Sheikh pushed in and held himself there while his thick semen poured into her. "Ya Allah, take all of me," he groaned. "All of me."

He saw Queenie nod up at him almost unconsciously, her legs wrapping themselves around his ass and holding him inside her as he pumped his seed into her depths. There was no conflict, no doubt, no holding back. It seemed natural and easy, the Sheikh thought as he pushed out the last of his load and then lowered his head against her neck in satisfied exhaustion.

Could it really be as simple as this, he thought as he kissed her neck gently and smiled against her skin. An awful marriage ends, and something wonderful begins. She will get pregnant from my seed tonight. We will be married within a year. She will sit beside me on the throne. We will have more children, grow old together. And when we die, we will race through the skies together, hand in hand, escorted by God's angels to His heaven. It is perfect, is it not? How can it be so perfect?

"Because we both deserve it," he said out loud to her, completing his thoughts in speech. She looked up at him, nodding as if she'd somehow been following along in her own mind, as if her own thoughts had been tracking with his. "Our private journeys have led us to each other, and now that we have found one another, there is no doubt."

"No doubt," she whispered back, and in her faraway look the Sheikh could see that he was right. This woman had been to hell and back in her own private journey, and although he knew little of her life and her past, the mystery only made his heart leap with delight at how much fun it would be to discover who this woman was, what she liked, what she hated, what she looked like in the morning, whether she snored in her sleep. "None at all."

12

"**N**ot at all," the Sheikh said, grinning as Queenie sat across from him at the breakfast table. "I did not hear a thing."

"So I don't snore. That's good," Queenie said, blushing as she looked into his eyes and then at the sturdy teakwood table that was laden with breakfast flatbreads, camel-milk cheese, finely ground hummus, an array of fresh fruit, chopped nuts. There were also some steaming hot dishes that looked savory and delicious. "You do, though."

"Excuse me?" the Sheikh said, raising an eyebrow and glancing at her as an attendant poured out two cups of hot sweet tea. "I do what?"

"Snore. Sounds like a chainsaw. We might have to sleep in separate bedrooms from now on."

The Sheikh waved away his attendant and glared across the table at Queenie. "Our first morning together and already you are complaining. Usually a woman waits at least a year after marriage before pointing out faults in her husband."

Queenie's heart skipped a beat and then began to pound like a drum as she stared at the Sheikh. He'd just talked about them being married! And he'd said it so casually, like it was a foregone conclusion, a done deal! What was happening here? Was she still hallucinating? Had some strange cosmic shift occurred on Christmas Day, and now everyone in the world had their Christmas wishes coming true?

I want him, she'd wished on Christmas Eve. Now here he was, calmly sipping his tea, glaring at her playfully across the breakfast table as she complained about him snoring!

"A woman waits a year after marriage to begin complaining?" she said, cocking her head and reaching for the silver cup of steaming tea. "What is this, the 1920s?"

"You wish!" said the Sheikh. "The rules governing what a woman may or may not do in Wakhrani are more reminiscent of the Middle Ages than the 1920s."

Queenie snorted into her tea, hurriedly putting the cup back down before she spilled it all over as she giggled. "Is that why your wife left?" she said, the words coming out before she could stop them. Oh, God, what did she just say?! Oh, God, he was gonna kick her out on her ass!

The Sheikh hesitated for a moment, but then he took another sip of his tea and leaned back in the hand-carved teakwood chair. "Renita left because Renita was never really here. The marriage was official, but never real. We were never meant to be with one another, and only after our parents died did we have the courage to face the truth and end it."

Queenie closed her eyes and took a breath. "I'm sorry. I don't know why I asked you that. It's none of my business."

"Everything is your business from now on. We are together, and no question is off limits. What else do you want to know?"

Queenie exhaled slowly. This was happening, wasn't it? She was sitting here at the breakfast table with a king. His seed was still inside her, he'd casually implied that they were going to be married, and now he'd point-blank said they were together!

"Are we together?" she asked, blinking as she almost kicked herself for asking the question. "I mean . . ."

"Yes," he said, looking at her with those green eyes focused and steady. "We are together. Next question."

"But . . . but your wife. She said she was . . ." Queenie stammered, not sure if she was thrilled or terrified at how calm and resolute the Sheikh was right then. He'd already decided they were together. Decreed it. Ordered it. Whatever the right word was . . .

"Pregnant, yes. That is indeed what she said." Bawaar shrugged and snapped his fingers for an attendant to pour him another cup of tea. "And if she is, we will deal with it."

"You think she's lying?"

"Probably. But perhaps not. Regardless, it is of no consequence."

"How is your ex-wife being pregnant with your child and heir of no consequence?" Queenie said, frowning even though she was astounded at how openly they were talking about matters that seemed like . . . well, that seemed like they *shouldn't* be talked about this early in a relationship! Had they just skipped like three years ahead in one night?

The Sheikh held his steady look. "Renita might be carrying my child, but she is not carrying my heir. You are carrying my heir."

Queenie almost choked on her flatbread-and-hummus breakfast sandwich as she stared into the Sheikh's eyes. So they'd met a week earlier in an elevator. Then a kiss beneath the mistletoe. One kidnapping. A night in bed together. And now they were talking about marriage, babies, and how to handle his psycho ex-wife. No way this was real. Not even *Mills and Boon* would dare to put such a ridiculous story out there because no one would ever believe it!

But you believe it, don't you, Queenie told herself as she glanced around the sprawling open room where they were being served breakfast by silent, perfectly groomed attendants. You believe *him*, don't you? When he said we've found each other because we deserve each other . . . you believe it too, don't you?

Maybe it is that simple, Queenie wondered as she took in the sight of the yellow sandstone walls bathed in sunlight, smelled the clean, dry air that floated in from the open desert beyond the balcony, listened to the distant prayer call from the city of Wakhrani. Yup, maybe it is that simple. Maybe my happily-ever-after really is here. My journey prepared me for this moment, for this man, for this life, and it's the same with him. We skipped the awkwardness and tension of "dating" and "getting to know ya" and jumped right into the "we're together now, and so all we have to do is figure out the details" phase.

Is that even a phase, Queenie wondered as she thought back to the men in her life. Boys, really. She'd had a lot of sex, but there'd never been a real boyfriend until all that drama with her blue-eyed lottery winner, her prince who'd been a frog in disguise.

Then suddenly doubt whipped through Queenie as reality peeked through the fluffy clouds of happiness that had enveloped her ever since she'd woken up beside the man she'd casually wished for on Christmas morning. Reality, which reminded her that this man knew nothing of her past, and if—or when—he decided to ask, she'd have to be honest. And then what? What of all this talk of marriage and being together and carrying his heir? This man was a *king*! Soon reality would break through to him as well, bringing him face to face with the truth that she was way beneath him, that the fascination with her was just one hell of a rebound, a reaction to the drama his ex-wife was throwing at him. Once that was done, so was Queenie!

Queenie swallowed hard as a chill rose up along her back. She shifted in her chair, suddenly feeling uncomfortable . . . uncomfortable with everything: herself, this place, this man, this entire damned situation. A part of her wanted to get up and run, to shut this down before it got too far, before she was swept away with the romance of it, before she actually believed a girl like her could end up with a guy like him.

When does that *ever* happen in real life, Queenie wondered as her jaw tightened. Sure, bosses fuck cleaning ladies all over America. Kings have been boinking scullery-maids since the Middle Ages. But what happens next? When does it ever end well for the maid?

"What's the plan here?" she asked, closing her eyes

and facing him, her boldness surprising her even as that annoying sense of dread kept climbing up her spine like a ten-legged insect.

"What do you mean?" said the Sheikh, sipping his tea and leaning back again.

"I mean, we've known each other for a few days, and you're saying we're together now. Forgive me if I find that hard to believe. So if this is just a wham-bam-no-thank-you-ma'am, then you need to let me know now and I'll just pack my bags and get back to my life."

"You have no bags," said the Sheikh, his green eyes twinkling through the steam rising above his teacup. "I kidnapped you, remember?"

"Oh, yes. Of course."

"And that means you are my captive. So no, you are not free to get back to your life unless I release you." He paused, his eyes twinkling again before they narrowed. "Do you *want* to get back to your life? The life you had before Christmas Eve? Before the mistletoe? Before me?"

Queenie blinked as she felt herself getting pulled in by his cool confidence, his calm sense of assuredness. Who was this man? Why was he so damned interested in her?

"Why me?" she asked without thinking. "Why pick me?"

Bawaar shrugged. "Why not?"

Queenie blinked as the depth of his simple question hit her square in the heart, making her breathless, almost knocking her out. "Because . . ." she started to say before realizing that if she said any more, it would basically mean she was trying to convince him *not* to choose her! Was she that insecure? Was he testing her? Challenging her? Asking her to find it in herself to believe that she was on par with a king, worthy of a Sheikh, meant to be with him?

"All right, listen," Bawaar said, lowering his teacup and leaning forward. He reached out and grabbed her hand, the touch sending a spark of heat through Queenie's body. "You want to know the plan? The truth is there was no plan. The attraction was real. The moment I saw you in that elevator, I wanted you. Perhaps it was because my divorce had been finalized and something had opened up in me. Perhaps it was because I spent my entire life forcing myself into staying loyal to a woman that did not arouse me sexually, that did not call to my body the way you did." He paused, swallowing hard and exhaling. "And yes, perhaps it is a rebound of sorts. Perhaps I would have felt this way about any woman I bumped into on the elevator. Maybe it was the timing and not the woman." He shook his head and smiled. "But that is just logic talking, and neither the heart nor the body cares about logic. My heart tells me it is about you and not the situation. And by Allah, my body backs up my heart. So to hell with logic and common sense. If there was no plan before, we will make a plan now."

Queenie stared at Bawaar, losing herself in his gaze as she felt him stroke her hand with a firm gentleness that gave her goosebumps. She felt herself nodding, then smiling, and finally she was giggling as she realized that of *course* she was willing to give this a shot! Worst case he'd break her heart and she'd never see him again. Wasn't that worth the risk? In it to win it, yeah? No shame. No guilt. She'd already opened her legs for him, and now she was hesitating to open her heart? If she walked away now, it only proved that she *was* a whore, right? It would only prove what her mother, her teachers, and everyone in school said about her. Only a whore spreads her legs for a man while keeping her heart locked tight. How was that for some logic?!

"All right," she said softly. "Let's make a plan."

13

"Here is the plan," said the Sheikh, stroking Queenie's arm and looking into her eyes. He was making this up as he went along, but he felt a calm confidence that was intoxicating as he heard the words roll off his tongue. "We will be married. You will bear my child. That way, if Renita truly is pregnant with my child, it will be no matter because I will make sure the laws say that the child born in wedlock will be the true heir to Wakhrani. Our child, Queenie." He paused and frowned, a chill running through him as the pieces suddenly fell into place. "But our marriage will need to be secret. And your pregnancy will need to be an even bigger secret."

Queenie's eyes widened, and the Sheikh felt her breath catch. "Why?" she said, her voice soft and urgent, her tone telling the Sheikh that she already understood why. "Are you saying what I think you're saying?"

Bawaar nodded. He hadn't really considered it until now, but after seeing Renita face to face at that party, he knew she was capable of anything. And showing up with Anders Van Hosen, the head of a security agency with a reputation for doing more than just simple "protection" . . . ya Allah, Renita was sending a message, wasn't she?

Take me back, or I'll take your kingdom.

The Sheikh's head spun as the scenarios played out in his mind. Could it be that Renita didn't realize she was pregnant until after the divorce? That was the only thing that made sense, or else she would have told him about the child before he signed the papers. She would have tried to get him to give it another try for the sake of their unborn child, the heir of Wakhrani.

Unless she was afraid that I would have divorced her anyway, disowned the child, perhaps even done something more drastic to her and the baby, the Sheikh thought as his jaw tightened and his head began to pound. Perhaps that public scene was carefully planned to protect herself, to make sure that if she suddenly disappeared, all fingers would point to me as the culprit! Ya Allah, she is smart! She could have kept the baby a secret from me until she gave birth. She could have had me killed—the Van Hosens were more than capable of that—and then her child would be the heir to Wakhrani, making her the Queen Mother by default!

So why not do that? Does she truly believe I would take her back? Or is she just unhinged, playing a game that even I do not understand yet?

"What's going on in there?" came Queenie's voice. "What are you thinking about, Bawaar? Let me in there. Talk to me."

The Sheikh took a long, controlled breath. Then he shook his head. "It is possible I made a mistake," he said softly. "It is irresponsible and selfish for me to bring you into this. It is too dangerous. You are not ready for this. I am sorry."

"Wait, what?" Queenie said, pulling her hand away from his, her eyes narrowing in anger. "You already have brought me into this! You kissed me, kidnapped me, fucked me, and now you're saying I'm not ready for this! I'm *in* this, Bawaar." She snorted, tossing her hair back and shaking her head. "And if you think I'm not ready for this . . . whatever it is . . . well, then you don't know anything about me."

Bawaar smiled. "Perhaps I do not. So tell me something more about you."

"Oh, so now we're doing the getting-to-know-you bit? All right. Shoot. Ask me anything."

"Did you grow up in Texas?" he asked.

"Alaska. Juno."

The Sheikh's eyes widened. "Alaska! A desert of ice and snow!"

"Something like that," Queenie said, a smile slowly forming on her face. "What else do you wanna know? Favorite color? Favorite food? Go on."

"Why did you leave Alaska?" he asked. "Certainly it was not to pursue more promising career opportunities in Texas."

"Considering I'm a janitor? I guess not. I left because . . ." She blinked and shrugged. "Let's just say it was becoming too dangerous for everyone else in my life."

The Sheikh grinned. "So you like danger?"

Queenie shrugged. "I like risk, I suppose. Considering I'm still here, still talking to you, still smiling."

Bawaar reached for her hand again, but Queenie pulled away from him, biting her lip and smiling in a way that made him harden beneath his black silk pajamas. He wanted to ask her more, ask her what she meant by her answers. But he held off. In a way he did not want to know. This woman had clearly left Alaska to escape something—perhaps to escape herself. A man? A crime? Both? It did not matter. If and when it did matter, she would tell him, he was sure of it. For now, he did not care about her past. It meant nothing to him.

"You are indeed still smiling," he whispered, moving his chair closer and reaching for her hand again.

But she swatted him away, crossing her arms over her breasts defiantly. He grinned and leaned back, holding his hands up in a gesture of mock surrender. "So all right. I will lay it out there. Here is the situation: Wakhrani's laws of ascendancy have some interesting clauses, and I believe Renita is well aware of them and is looking to play them to perfection. Of course, I am king and I could simply change the laws, but it is a long process, and Renita could take it up with the Pan-Arabic Council and delay things."

"Go on," Queenie said, her arms still crossed over her breasts.

"The way it works is that the Sheikh's first born child is heir to the throne. There is no question of legitimacy. For example, if the Sheikh gets a harem-girl pregnant before any of his wives bear his child, the bastard child will have claim to the throne."

Queenie frowned. "Sounds pretty equal-opportunity. Also a good way to keep the Sheikh's cock in line, right? If I remember my historical romance novels, back in England and Europe, the king could spread his seed far and wide, but the bastard children would never have a higher claim to the throne if there were any children born in wedlock."

The Sheikh laughed. "Yes, the rule was put into place by my father's four wives."

"Convenient," said Queenie. "So you had four mothers?"

"Yes. You could say that."

"Well, that figures."

Bawaar frowned. "What do you mean?"

Queenie shrugged. "Well, I'm not a psychiatrist, but you display a strange mix of deep respect and loyalty towards women—for example, you said you never once cheated on your wife, even though you could have easily done it without anyone knowing. But at the same time, there is a need in you to assert control over women—perhaps a reaction to being controlled by women your entire life."

"Very impressive. That must be quite a training program we have in place for the custodians at Wakhrani Enterprises."

"My in-depth knowledge of psychology comes from reading romance novels. The hero is usually all messed up in the head by either his mother or an ex-lover. Then the heroine comes along and fixes him, even though he tries to deny that he's all fucked-up in the head. The end."

The Sheikh raised an eyebrow. Who in Allah's name was this woman? He eyed her up and down, his jaw tightening as his gaze rested on the swell of her breasts beneath the loose, flowing white robe she'd worn to bed. "So I demonstrate a need to control women?" he said softly, his eyes narrowing as he slowly stood up. "All right. I will grant you that. But you believe it is a reaction to being controlled by women my entire life? You do not think it is simply a

Mistletoe for the Sheikh

side-effect of being a king, a man in control of everything and everyone, including himself and his needs?"

Queenie snorted. "You're just proving my point. Remember how I said the hero always denies that he's messed up in the head? There you go. Denial."

"What about the heroine? She is never in denial? Never messed up in the head, as you say?"

"Sure she is. Always. And the fix for her is usually . . ." Queenie trailed off, glancing at the peak at the front of his black silk pajamas, her face going flush as she looked back up into his eyes. "You know, let's just eat. There's so much stuff here I want to try. What's that strange looking—"

"The fix for her is usually what?" said Bawaar, standing and stepping between Queenie and the table, putting his hands firmly on his hips and glancing down at her.

"Never stand between me and food in the morning," she said equally firmly, trying to reach around him for the breakfast flatbreads that were lending an exceptional aroma to the air.

"You want something to eat? Try this," grunted the Sheikh, pulling open the drawstring of his pajamas and letting them slide down past his thighs. His cock sprung out, filling itself to hardness as he looked down at her curves, her pretty round face, the way her mouth opened wide in shock as she glanced up at him and then squarely at the head of his manhood.

"You're disgusting," she said, giggling and swatting at his cock as he brought it close to her mouth. "Eww. Who does that?! That's not funny at all."

"Does it look like I am laughing?" Bawaar said, the arousal making his entire body stiffen as he stroked his erection to full hardness and then reached around and grabbed Queenie by the back of her neck, pulling her close. "I am simply being the man you said I was. A need to dominate and control women. Here we go. Now suck me. I command it. I require it. I damned well *order* it! Suck me, woman!"

Queenie kept her mouth firmly closed, raising an eyebrow and looking up at him. "My psychological analysis also said you have a deep-seated respect for women. Grabbing my neck and trying to shove your oversized cock down my throat doesn't quite fit the profile, you know."

"I will show you what doesn't quite fit," the Sheikh said, grinning devilishly as he pushed his cockhead up against her lips. "Come now. Open up, my queen."

Queenie tried to turn her head, but the Sheikh wouldn't let her. He coated her lips with his pre-cum, forcing himself into her mouth as she writhed under his grasp, half-giggling, half-sputtering. Finally she opened up, and the Sheikh pushed himself all the way into her mouth, groaning out loud when he felt her warmth envelop his shaft as her throat relaxed so he could slide all of himself into her.

"Ya Allah," he groaned. "You are good at this."

She pulled back and glared up at him, holding his wet shaft in her hand. "Excuse me?"

"It was a compliment!" said the Sheikh. "In over a decade of marriage, Renita sucked me off twice! And she complained all the way through it. She did not even let me come in her mouth!"

Queenie raised an eyebrow as she slowly moved his foreskin back and forth, reaching beneath for his balls and cupping them in her warm hands. "Are you seriously complaining about your ex-wife's skills while complimenting me on giving good blow-jobs? This is supposed to make me feel all warm and fuzzy inside?"

"Take me back in your mouth and I will make you feel warm and fuzzy inside, I guarantee it."

Queenie giggled as she stroked him. "Wow, you are one smooth-talking Sheikh. Though I'm not sure if I like the idea of feeling fuzzy inside. Not sure what that even means, to be honest."

"It is called poetic license. Please. Take me back into your mouth or I will come all over your face. I am so damned close already, woman."

Her grip on his shaft tightened, and she looked up at him, her eyes narrowed with mischief. "Now that's romantic. Suck me now or I'll come all over your face. I feel like I'm in a bad porno." Queenie twisted her mouth into a comical frown, looking off to her left as if deep in thought. "Not that there are any good pornos. So really, what I'm saying is—oh, *shit*!"

The Sheikh roared as he exploded all over her, her

touch bringing him to orgasm so quickly he couldn't hold himself back. He shouted again as he felt his balls tighten in her warm hands, his shaft flailing like a damned fireman's hose as he shot his semen all over her chin and neck, onto her clean white gown, into her hair even.

"Ya Allah!" he groaned as he pushed out the last of his load and then opened his eyes to see Queenie sitting before him, her eyes closed, her mouth half-open, a look of complete and utter shock on her pretty face.

"I . . . I can't even . . . oh, my *God* I can't believe you did that!" she sputtered, blinking as she let go of his spent cock and fumbled for a napkin. "You sick, twisted, *animal!*"

"I did not do that. *You* did it!" said the Sheikh, grinning as he grabbed a clean silk napkin and began to wipe the semen off her face. "Now sit still. Ya Allah, there is some in your hair."

"Oh, God, this is so sick," she groaned, keeping her eyes closed as the Sheikh carefully wiped her nose and cheeks and then tossed the napkin onto the table, reaching for a clean one. "Mama was right. I'm just a whore."

The Sheikh glanced down at her, frowning as he tried to figure out if she was serious. "Are you joking, or did your mother actually say that to you?"

Queenie blinked and carefully opened her eyes. "Both," she said after a moment. "I mean, I was joking, yeah. But Mama did say that to me." She rolled her eyes. "So did a lot of other people."

The Sheikh cleaned the last of his load off her smooth round face and then leaned in and kissed her gently on the lips. "Hey," he said softly. "That is not what I think of you. You understand that, yes?"

Queenie blinked, color rushing to her face. The Sheikh could tell his words mattered to her, and he kissed her again, deeper this time, a lingering kiss that said more than his words ever could.

She kissed him back, and then she pulled away and giggled. "Oh, Queenie," she said, mocking his voice. "You're not a whore. Here, let me clean my semen off your face."

The Sheikh laughed. "A king's semen is supposed to do wonders for the skin. And anyway, I have cleaned it all off. Your hair, however, is a different matter."

"Wait, you've got it all over my hair too? I'm gonna have to wash it out before it dries!"

Bawaar took a breath and nodded. "So you have some experience with this?"

Queenie glanced up at him, and the Sheikh knew he had gone too far. It meant nothing to him that she had been with other men before—indeed, if anything he was incredibly turned on by the idea of being with a woman who had some experience. Yes, he did have a need to be controlling and dominant in bed—a need that Renita had never come close to satisfying—but the truth remained that he did not have much experience outside of that loveless, mostly sexless marriage!

"I am sorry," he said softly, seeing the hurt on her face. "I did not mean . . . I mean, I do not care about . . . Queenie. *Queenie!*"

But she'd pushed her chair back and stormed out of the room, tears welling in her eyes as she clawed at her hair, shaking her head and muttering to herself. The Sheikh stared at her full figure, mesmerized by the way her bottom moved beneath the white silk gown. Then he sighed and shook his head, glancing down at his cock and closing his eyes.

There is still so much we have to learn about each other, he thought. So much we have to accept about each other . . . and ourselves. I am embarrassed about my lack of experience, just like she is ashamed about having too much experience! Does she not see that we are perfect for one another, that this is a match designed by Allah and the angels, that we are meant to fulfill the deepest needs of the other?

No, she does not see it yet, Bawaar thought as he strolled out of the day-chambers and towards the private baths of the Eastern Wing. You will need to show her.

"So go show her," he told himself, pulling off his tunic and walking through the halls stark naked, his cock filling out again as he heard the gush of the powerful shower-heads that he knew must be pouring warm water onto Queenie's luscious curves. "Show her that she has nothing to be ashamed about, that what she hates about herself is exactly what you love about her. Show her, Bawaar. Show her."

And at the same time show yourself to her. Show her your bare self. The man beneath the king. Open yourself up to her, give life to your deepest needs as a man, your darkest fantasies as a lover. You never dared to go there with Renita. Dare yourself to go there with Queenie. After all, if she is going to enter into this game, then you need to know she will stick with it, stay the course, stay with you no matter what. Otherwise what is the point? You might as well call Renita and simply ask her what she wants with this pregnancy thing!

The Sheikh heard the roar of the showers in the Royal Baths, and he smelled the bath soaps come through on the rising steam. He silently stepped through the door, noting that it had been left partly open, and stood outside the arched doorway made of translucent glass that separated the showers from the changing area. Queenie's clothes lay in a crumpled mess on the smooth sandstone floor, and the Sheikh glanced down at himself. He was naked as the day he was born, and he smiled as he pushed open the door to the shower room.

14

"My compliments to the designer," Queenie said, looking through the steam of the showers and marveling at what lay beyond. Although three walls of the shower room were translucent glass, the fourth wall wasn't a wall at all—it was just open!

The showers opened to a private garden, perfectly manicured, indigenous dwarf palm-trees and desert shrubs rising up from the sandy soil. It looked like a cross between a desert paradise and a Japanese tea garden. It also made it seem like she was bathing in the open, perhaps in a waterfall, maybe in the rain.

"Compliment accepted," the Sheikh said from behind her, his arms sliding around her waist, which was slick from the coconut-milk soap that Queenie thought smelled absolutely divine.

She'd heard him come in. Indeed, she'd expected him to follow her. She giggled as his hand rubbed her belly, moved down along her wide hips, around to her dark triangle, which was wet with suds. She felt his fingers search out her slit, and she gasped and leaned back into his hard body as he thumbed her clit while curling two fingers inside her.

"Wait, you designed this? It's pretty bold. Open." She paused, gasping as she felt the Sheikh's cock rise against her naked rump. "What did your wife think?"

She felt him tense up for a moment, and indeed, she was almost surprised at herself for asking the question so casually. But it seemed appropriate. After all, if she was going to step into this man's life, she needed to know about her adversary, yes? In it to win it, right?

"She never used it. Not once. She thought it was disgusting, to be naked and exposed to the light of day," whispered the Sheikh, his right arm moving up along her stomach and firmly closing on her breast, squeezing so hard it made her moan.

The Sheikh's other hand was driving firmly into her pussy, his cock hard and full, lined up along her rear crack. Queenie sighed and rubbed her ass against him as her arousal flowed like the warm waters of the six showerheads.

"So you designed this for her," she whispered. "To help her open up." She paused, feeling the Sheikh tense up again. But he also hardened against her buttocks as she spoke, and so she continued. "To help open both of you up, perhaps?"

The Sheikh pinched her nipple so hard Queenie winced in pain, groaning as the fingers of his other hand drove into her pussy at a frenzied pace, making her dizzy with arousal as she smelled the warm coconut milk soap and shampoo, stared through clouds of steam at the private Arabian garden of fantasy. Private fantasy. His fantasy. A fantasy that his wife had never indulged, never given life to, never made real.

"What is your fantasy?" she whispered. "Tell me."

The Sheikh kissed her neck hard, bringing his fingers out from between her legs and swapping hands so he could play with her other breast while fingering her. "It is perhaps a bit early in our relationship to go there."

Queenie giggled, trying to turn and see his face. But his hold on her was too firm, and so she stayed pressed up against his body, facing out to the open garden, letting the trees and shrubs watch her in the flesh. "You've already asked me to marry you and carry your child just to thwart your evil ex-wife from seizing your kingdom. Then you fucked me, came on my face, and now we're showering together in the open air. I think we've left behind any traditional ideas of how a relationship is supposed to proceed. Don't you think?"

The Sheikh grunted against her neck. "Has this not been a traditional courtship thus far? I did kiss you under the mistletoe, just as tradition demands. And once I did that, I was bound to marry you. In a way, I am following the most conservative traditions of any culture, anywhere! To kiss a woman means to claim her."

"So I've been claimed, huh? Based on tradition and propriety? And this has nothing to do with your ex-wife and whatever she's trying to pull on you?"

Queenie could sense the Sheikh's frown even though she couldn't see his face.

"Is that what you think?" he said, grinding his cock against her ass, his thick shaft slowly spreading her soft rear cheeks. "That all of this is because of my wife?"

"In a way, yes. I think I arouse you because you sense I can give you something she couldn't—or wouldn't—I don't know which." Queenie paused as she felt the Sheikh's fingers slow their relentless drive into her. "I also think you sense that I'd be willing to do whatever it takes to counter Renita's plan—whatever that might be."

The Sheikh was silent for a long moment, and Queenie wondered if she'd said too much. Was she being too bold? Too forward? Too aggressive? Too . .

. desperate? Was he turned off by her willingness to jump into bed with him . . . jump into *everything* with him?!

And why was she doing it, anyway? Was it his money? His power? The romance of royalty? The danger?

Or was it just the way he made her feel . . .

She moaned as she suddenly became intensely aware of his fingers curling up inside her most secret space, and then she was coming, the orgasm storming in out of nowhere. She shouted in shock as the climax whipped through her body, making her hunch over as the Sheikh held her, his fingers still driving into her.

"Oh, God," she whimpered, her eyelids fluttering as splinters of that private garden came through her vision while she came in the Sheikh's arms. Her mind was a mess, her body soaked and dripping, but those thoughts kept swirling in her mind as she stared at the garden.

Why was she here? What was *her* game? Was this the move of a woman who could tell this was the best man she could land and so she was going all in? No shame in that. Every woman thought like that, even if no one would admit it even to their besties. But was there something more that was pulling her into this, into him, into this situation that was ambiguous and messy at best, downright dangerous at worst?

The sunlight sparkled from the grains of sand in the

Mistletoe for the Sheikh

garden, and Queenie squinted as her climax wound its way down. So bright, she thought. Like sparks. Flames. Fire.

Oh, God, that's at the core of this, isn't it? This whole situation is fire! This whole situation is a burning house! And that's why I can't stay away! I want to be in the middle of it, standing there with a matchbook in my hands, giggling like a madwoman as my king holds me close! This is my whole life coming together in one blazing hot climax! All those years of reading those books. All those times playing with fire. This is the inferno that brings all of it to a close!

And either it'll be a happy ending, or it'll all go down in flames.

15

Her hair looked like flames in the sun, the Sheikh thought as he felt her convulse against his body, her orgasm taking him by surprise at first. But he'd held onto her, the two of them facing the garden, that space which he'd designed to be open yet private, just like the Sheikh had always envisioned a true marriage to be.

Open but private.

Ya Allah, the Sheikh thought as he kissed her cheek from behind and slowly pulled his fingers out of her. That describes this woman perfectly, does it not? She has been open and honest with me, but yet she holds things close, keeps a part of herself private and hidden. Just like fire ... you can see it clearly, but if you get too close you will burn.

And perhaps that is just what I need. A woman who will stand by me no matter what, no matter what needs to happen, no matter what needs to be done.

A chill went through the Sheikh even though the water was hot and the sun was high in the desert sky. He could see that there was both light and darkness in this woman, bright sun and storm clouds. She'd clearly left Alaska to get away from something. Perhaps to get away from herself? No. This woman was not running from herself. She accepted herself, accepted who she was. That was why she'd boldly agreed to go along with him, trusting her instincts, trusting her body, trusting her own sense of adventure. So what was it?

"What was it?" he asked, blurting out the words suddenly, as if his thoughts had burst into speech without his intention.

"What was what?" she said.

"What made you run? Why did you leave Alaska?"

Queenie was quiet for a moment, as if she was debating whether to be open or stay private, shine like the sun or stay obscured in clouds.

"Long answer or short answer?" she said finally.

"Well," said the Sheikh, reaching for the coconut-milk shampoo on the coated wooden shelf to his left, "we still need to wash your hair, so long answer."

She was silent again as the Sheikh gently lathered the shampoo into her thick brown hair, placing his palm across her forehead so it wouldn't get into her eyes. "Let's just say it was getting a little hot for me up there in the Arctic Circle."

The Sheikh frowned as he considered her choice of words. "Heat," he said finally. "You mean the police? You did something?"

Queenie snorted. "Oh, I did a *lot* of things."

"Illegal things?"

"I consider the law to be simply a set of suggestions," Queenie said. "I generally do what I want, and if it breaks the law, then whoops!"

The Sheikh laughed. "When you are a Sheikha, you can make the laws yourself. How does that sound?"

"Boring," she said with a giggle. "What's the fun in that? It would mean that everything I wanna do is within the rules!"

"Ah, so you find pleasure in breaking rules. Flaunting authority. Ignoring Mother's pleas. Disobeying Father's wishes," the Sheikh whispered as he felt himself stiffen to full mast again, though he'd been hard for a long time now.

"Something like that," she muttered. "Though I never even met my father. So maybe that's the root of it all. Maybe I just need that authoritative male figure to put his foot down, put me in my place, take control, dominate me."

The Sheikh almost exploded against her lower back and ass when he heard her words. Was she playing him, he wondered as he finished lathering her hair and took a step back, pulling her into the central meeting point of all the shower streams. If she was, she was doing it perfectly. Telling him exactly what he wanted to hear. Saying things she knew his ex-wife would never have said.

Does she think she needs to compete with Renita, he wondered as he watched the water roll down her naked shoulders in beads as he stood behind her, the sun shining through the open wall. Ya Allah, if only she knew that even at the best of times I was barely attracted to Renita. That woman is no competition to this one. But there is no need to tell Queenie that yet. Let it play out. Let us see what this woman is willing to do to win her king. Let us see what she is willing to take.

"So you were a bad girl growing up in Alaska," he whispered, turning off the showers one by one until the bathroom slowly went quiet.

"Very bad," she whispered, rubbing her ass against him and giggling. "May I have a towel please."

"No towels for bad girls," he said, reaching around and pinching her wet nipples until they hardened into points. "The sun will dry you. Come into my garden."

"Um, sunburn, anyone?" she said, squinting as he led her out through the open wall and onto the fine sand of the private garden. "I don't think so!"

"I will do this in the shade. And though you will feel the burn, it will not be from the sun."

Queenie whipped her head around as the Sheikh tightened his grip around her waist, pulling her out into the sunshine. "Excuse me? Do what in the shade?"

"Show you what happens to bad girls who have no sense of discipline," he said, grinning as he led her to the shade of a palm tree and pointed at the ground. "Down on your knees, please."

"Um, I don't think so. Not until you tell me what you're going to do!"

The Sheikh reached down and rubbed her naked ass, which was still wet from the shower. This would sting, he knew, feeling his cock throb as he imagined her magnificent globes turning red as he spanked her, indulging himself in a fantasy he'd had for years—a fantasy he'd never lived out. The strange thing was, even when he'd closed his eyes and imagined it, it had never been Renita in that fantasy. It had always been a woman whose face was obscured. Nothing but her curves, the back of her head, her clean, tight asshole staring at him as he spanked her raw and then took his release. Was it Queenie who'd always been in his fantasies? Or was it the other way around? Was the initial attraction to Queenie simply because she resembled that faceless woman of his most private fantasies?

Ya Allah, I am a sick man, he thought as he put his big hands on her shoulders and pushed her down to the ground. She resisted at first, but when she half-turned and glanced down at his cock, which was sticking straight out, brown and glistening in the sun, she fluttered her eyelids and obeyed.

Perhaps she will tolerate me for a while and then call me a monster and leave, he thought as he made her lean forward and stick her ass up in the air. She had to know what was coming, yes? And although there was hesitation, she was submitting. Allowing him to dominate. Giving life to his fantasy like she knew it was what he needed.

"Have you ever been spanked?" he whispered, leaning in and kissing her smooth asscheeks, running his tongue along the perfect outer curve of her crack.

Queenie shook her head slowly, her breathing sounding heavy and labored. He could smell her wetness starting to flow from between her legs, and he reached beneath her and rubbed her mound until his hand was soaked with her discharge.

"Never allowed it," she said softly. "One guy tried it and I kicked him in the balls. Most of the others were too timid to even . . . oh, God, what are you doing?"

The Sheikh slid his middle finger deep into her asshole as she spoke, the wetness he'd gathered from her pussy making a wonderful natural lubricant. "Go on," he whispered, pushing the finger in down to the knuckle and holding it still as he felt her tense up and then slowly begin to relax. "You were saying?"

"I . . . I don't know what I was saying," she whimpered.

"I believe you threatened to kick me in the balls if I attempted to spank you," the Sheikh said, staring at the sight of her rear pucker closing around his finger. It was exquisite, erotic, beautiful. Better than his wildest fantasy, and this was just the beginning! "That sort of statement calls for a higher level of discipline than I anticipated. A much deeper level of domination."

He moved his finger in slow circles as he spoke, feeling her anus relax and open up enough to slide another finger into her. His cock was pumped full of blood, throbbing like it was begging to enter her. But he held off, smiling as the swaying palm leaves filtered the sun, casting splinters of shadow on Queenie's smooth white skin.

With two fingers in her asshole, he brought his other hand down on her left asscheek, a tight, quick slap that made her cry out in surprise. He massaged her rump, then slapped her again on her rear cushion, his breath catching when he saw her buttocks begin to turn red.

"Oh, fuck," she groaned after taking several deep gulps of air. "That's just . . . oh, God, that's just . . ."

"Have you ever fantasized about this?" he whispered, spanking her once more, harder this time, his open palm getting her squarely on the meat of her rump, making her ass shiver and shake.

She cried out again, shaking her head and then nodding. "Yeah," she finally said. "I used to read some Victorian romances, and there was some spanking in there. Powerful men disciplining defiant women sort of thing. But . . . I mean . . ."

"But yet you never allowed a man to do that to you," the Sheikh said, pulling his fingers out of her asshole and spanking her other rear cheek so hard a bird peeked its head out from the palm leaves, chirped at them, and then flew away. "Why not?"

Queenie didn't answer, and the Sheikh leaned forward and kissed her lower back, his cock resting lengthwise against her rear crack. He didn't ask the question again. He already knew the answer. This woman was strong and dominant in her own way. She would never allow a less dominant man to impose himself on her. And so many men were goddamn pussies these days. Unwilling to let go, to dominate their woman the way she craved in her private fantasies. The Sheikh knew this because he'd been a man like that throughout his marriage—holding himself back. He'd married the wrong woman, and then he'd doubled down on his mistake by staying in the marriage. No more. Not this time. This woman was not a mistake, and he knew it because this time he'd followed his cock and his heart, not logic or the advice of his dead mothers.

A wave of anger whipped through the Sheikh as he thought back to how his mother and stepmothers had arranged the marriage with Renita, convincing the eighteen-year-old Bawaar that she was the right one for him. He'd felt nothing at that first meeting with the frigid Arabian minor princess from one of the neighboring Sheikhdoms. And on the wedding night he'd almost been sick to his stomach when he realized he had a lifetime of unfulfilling sex to look forward to—unless he took more wives or chose to get sex from whores.

Taking more than one wife was a non-starter—his mother and step-mothers had made sure of that. They'd changed the laws of Wakhrani after Bawaar's father had died, and although Bawaar could have reinstated the old traditions when he ascended to the throne, he did not. He'd seen what having four wives had done to his father. He'd experienced what having four mothers had done to him! Ya Allah, imagine being saddled with four Renitas, he'd thought, with all of them scheming and conspiring against him!

And so Bawaar had turned his attention to his work, his duty, his kingdom and people. He'd modernized the economy, positioning Wakhrani to eventually move away from relying on oil revenues. He'd done away with archaic laws while still maintaining the good and useful traditions that came from the

Mistletoe for the Sheikh

kingdom's Islamic heritage. And he'd dutifully tried to impregnate his Queen, to make sure the line continued when he was gone.

The Sheikh reached around and pressed Queenie's breasts as he grinded his cock against her rear, closing his eyes and groaning out loud as he felt the splintered sunlight on his bare shoulders. It was like he was letting go of the past as he slowly took this new woman into his life, and it was only as he allowed himself to sink deeper into his mind that he recognized how much of an impact the lack of children had had on him.

After ten years without a royal pregnancy, certainly rumors had spread throughout the kingdom. Was the Sheikha barren? Was the Sheikh impotent? Was there something else going on? It didn't make sense. The Sheikh had privately gotten himself tested, and the results had clearly shown a healthy sperm-count with strong swimmers! Renita herself had refused to take any tests, and she'd almost spat at him when he suggested fertility treatments.

Bawaar had considered having Renita secretly tested, perhaps by having one of her attendants draw blood from her while she was asleep. He'd wondered if she was taking contraceptives. It seemed to be the only explanation. After all, in ten years there would at least have been a miscarriage, yes? Unless she'd had one and kept it a secret!

There had been a phase when Bawaar wondered

if Renita had in fact been getting pregnant but was aborting his children, but he'd finally dismissed it as paranoia. After all, although no one who knew her would classify Renita as having maternal instincts, the woman most certainly would want her child in line for the throne, yes? Renita herself was a minor Jordanian princess, with no chance of sitting on a throne in her home kingdom. And certainly she'd enjoyed the pomp and splendor that went along with being a Sheikha. In fact that seemed to be the only thing that brought a smile to Renita's face through most of their marriage.

"Why didn't you guys have children in all those years you were married?" Queenie asked, and the Sheikh opened his eyes and stared at the back of her head, wondering if he was imagining the question.

"Are you asking if there is something wrong with me?" the Sheikh growled after getting over the shock at her strangely timed question. "You dare question the king's virility?"

Queenie laughed from beneath him. "Well, considering I saw your virility up close and personal when you exploded all over my face and hair, no. I'm just questioning . . . I guess I'm just curious. Is that why you left her? Because she couldn't have children? And that's why you think she's lying about being pregnant?"

The Sheikh felt a chill rise up in him along with a

spark of anger. Was she asking if he discarded his wife because of an inability to have children?! He clenched his fist, resisting the urge to spank her so hard she cried for mercy. But then he closed his eyes and acknowledged the truth: That he'd asked himself that same question in the years leading up to the divorce.

Is it true? Am I a man who saw his wife as nothing more than a tool, a vehicle to continue my line? And once it appeared that Renita either could not or would not carry my child, I decided to leave her?

"Do you think I will leave you if you cannot bear me a child?" he asked. "Is that why you are asking?"

He felt her tense up beneath him, and then she turned and looked at him. "So are we together now? Is that why we're talking about the conditions under which you'll leave me?" She smiled and then shook her head again. "No. I guess it sounds like I'm asking because I'm worried about you dumping me if I can't pop out an heir for your royal line. But really, I don't think you'll leave me."

The Sheikh's eyes widened, and he couldn't help but smile back at this American woman. Ya Allah, she was a . . . janitor?! The king and the cleaning lady?! Where did she get such confidence? Was it confidence or recklessness?

"That is a little presumptuous, do you not think?" he said softly, his voice deepening as he held the eye contact until she finally blinked and looked down.

"We have only just met. Perhaps I will meet someone else next week."

"Fine with me," she said, shaking her ass in his face and shrugging. "You can have up to four wives, right? What the hell. Maybe the other bitches can carry your children. That way my pussy won't get all stretched out."

The Sheikh almost choked with laughter as he listened to Queenie up the ante, match him blow for blow as they joked about matters that might have made any other woman pout, sulk, or throw an epic tantrum. Ya Allah, this was just what he needed to offset the schemes and machinations of whatever Renita was planning. This was just what he needed from a queen.

"Having other wives might save you from the pain of childbirth," said the Sheikh, reaching between her legs from behind and rubbing her wet slit as she giggled and then moaned. "But you are still going to get stretched like never before."

"Delusions of grandeur," she muttered as the Sheikh pressed the head of his cock against her slit and began to push. "Oh, God, what is that? It's so . . . so *big*!"

The Sheikh roared with laughter, pushing himself all the way into her warm vagina as she spread for him. He'd wanted to take her in the rear, dominate her in a way he'd never done with any woman. But now he wanted to pour his seed into her pussy again, fill her up all the way. He'd spanked her, held her down and pushed two fingers into her asshole, then spanked her again. But in the end she'd manipulated him with her humor and fire, a deadly combination that made him want to make babies with her, to plant his seed in her womb, to watch her push out children that had his eyes and her hair.

He came quickly, his balls seizing up and delivering his load deep into her cavern as she reached between them and rubbed him from beneath. Bawaar's eyes rolled up in his head when he felt her soft hands cup his balls and coax his semen out, and he pumped every last drop into her before collapsing on her back, his weight pushing her face-first into the soft sand.

"Did you come?" he asked after catching his breath and regaining some clarity of vision even though his head was still spinning from the orgasm.

She sighed from beneath him. "Since when does the king care if the chamber-maid has an orgasm?"

The Sheikh grunted. "I thought you were the cleaning lady."

"Chamber maid is much more dramatic. And lower down in the pecking order."

"You do not strike me as a high-drama woman. Nor do I think you worry much about society's pecking order," Bawaar said, rolling off her and sliding his hand between her legs. "Here. I will help you finish. Come."

She swatted his hand away, crossing her arms over

her boobs and making a face. "How romantic. First you come on my face. Then you spank me, violate my holiest of holes, and finally come inside me in like two seconds. My pleasure was clearly just an afterthought, and oh, now you want to shove your paws between my legs and make me come like you've got the magic touch."

"You should consider yourself fortunate I am thinking of your pleasure at all," the Sheikh said, grinning as he forced her thighs apart and rubbed her mound roughly. "As for my magic touch . . . that is absolutely real. Here. We shall test it. Let us see how long you can go without coming from my touch. Spread for me and I will show you that magic touch."

"No problem. I can hold my ground," Queenie said, keeping her arms folded over her boobs, a fake pout on her face. But she allowed the Sheikh to spread her thighs, and she closed her eyes as she felt the warm desert breeze whisper through her pubic curls as the sun moved along the desert sky. "I'll just think about baseball."

"Baseball? Does that arouse you? All those big bats and heavy balls? I can see why I make you think of that."

Queenie giggled, keeping her eyes clamped shut. "Keep talking. Your dumb jokes are gonna make sure my pussy dries up like a tomato in the sun."

"Now that is an arousing image," the Sheikh said

through stifled laughter, leaning over and watching his fingers part her slit, exposing her inner lips. "Did I mention I love to eat sundried tomatoes?"

"Eww!" Queenie shrieked as the Sheikh lowered his face, held her slit open, and began to lick her. "You're *so* gross!"

"This is only the beginning," the Sheikh said, licking his lips before going down again, this time finding her stiff clit and flicking it with the tip of his tongue. "Wait until you are pregnant and I am forced to take you in the arse every night. For the safety of the child, of course."

"Of course," she muttered, and Bawaar could see the arousal taking over. She was going to come soon, he knew. Good, because he was getting hard again. "Because your cock is so big that fucking me while I'm pregnant would impale our child. Keep dreaming, big shot."

"Did you just imply that I have a small cock?" the Sheikh said, grinning as he raised his head from between her legs. His erection was back, and he suddenly straddled her, moving up along her body until his cock stood straight out over her face. "All right. Open your eyes and tell me what you see. Open your eyes and bear witness to what is going to stretch your holiest of holes so wide it may never close up again. Open, I say!"

16

Queenie felt the shade on her face before she opened her eyes, and when she finally saw his cock standing straight above her like the Leaning Tower of Pisa, thick and curved, heavy and full, she gasped and swallowed hard.

"Just so you know," she said, moving her head to the left just so she could see past his massive cock, "I'm not taking another shower. My skin will get dried out and puckered."

"I'll get you puckered first," the Sheikh said, swatting her nose with his cock as she squealed in laughter.

"That doesn't even make sense! Where did you learn English?"

"Same place you did."

"Juno Elementary School?"

The Sheikh laughed. "I mean a combination of parents and television. I assume you were speaking some form of English before you started kindergarten, yes?"

"I think I was already reading before I started kindergarten," Queenie said, pushing herself up on her elbows and smiling. The palm leaves were moving gently in the warm breeze, the desert shrubs swaying in time, clear blue skies overhead, a bright yellow fireball of a sun that seemed to be smiling down at her. How perfect was this?! How perfect was *he*?! It seemed like they'd known each other forever, the way they were just hanging out in a garden, naked, teasing, flirting . . . just *being*! It really seemed like they were somewhere nothing could touch them, nothing could reach them, nothing could—

A harsh buzz suddenly sounded from one of the desert shrubs towards the Sheikh's left. He raised an eyebrow and turned to it. The buzz came again, and Queenie realized it was an alarm or bell of some kind hidden in the plant!

"What the hell is that?" she said, watching as the Sheikh sighed and then crawled over to the shrub. She stared as Bawaar poked around in the bush, reached his hand in there, and pulled out a red phone. "OK, you gotta be kidding me! Is that an intercom or something? How did your people know we were here?"

"They did not," he said calmly. "There are red intercoms in every room and private space in the Palace." He put the phone to his ear and shrugged, glancing at her naked breasts and winking. "I am a king. Ruler of a nation. I have to be available and reachable at all times, Queenie."

Queenie nodded, glancing at his cock, noticing that as he spoke in Arabic on the phone, clearly his attention was being pulled to other matters. She sighed and looked around for her clothes—or *any* clothes. Nothing. Finally she glanced back towards the Royal Baths. There must be towels in there, she thought, standing and making her way back indoors.

But then she stopped, frowning and turning when she heard the anger in the Sheikh's voice. She couldn't understand what he was saying, but she understood enough to know that it was serious.

"Iidha kunt tatahadath alearabiat, aismahuu li 'an 'aerif," he said.

Then he tossed the phone at the bush, glaring at the plant as if it was to blame for whatever national emergency had warranted a call on the red phone.

"Trouble in paradise?" Queenie said, smiling hopefully even though she could see that Bawaar was not in the mood for jokes. "What's wrong? Are the Americans invading? Do you need me to run out there naked with an American flag and tell them it's OK?"

The Sheikh forced a chuckle. "They will probably assume you are a suicide bomber."

"A naked suicide bomber?" Queenie said, her hands on her hips, head cocked to one side. "And where would I hide the bomb, genius?"

The Sheikh glanced down along her body, his green eyes narrowing. "I have some ideas," he said softly.

Queenie's mouth opened wide with indignation, but she could see that despite their fun back-and-forth, there was something else going on in the Sheikh's world that demanded his attention. She turned towards the Royal Baths once again, thinking about those towels. But then she turned back to him, frowning and blinking as she realized that hey, this was her world too now. After all, he'd said they were together, and she'd already decided she was in this to win this.

So don't turn away when he's got something to deal with, she told herself, swallowing hard as she took a step toward the Sheikh. You want to be his woman? You want to be his partner? You want to be his queen? Then don't walk away when something serious comes up! Walk *to* him, not *away* from him!

"How can I help?" she said softly. "What do you need me to do?"

The Sheikh blinked, a half-smile coming to his face. But it was a strange smile, like he was confused—not about her, but about whatever he'd been told on that red phone.

"I think you have already done it," he said finally,

rubbing his stubble and walking up to her. He took her arm and led her back towards the Royal Baths. "That was my minister of Public Relations. Renita has just announced to the press that although she is pregnant with the heir of Wakhrani, she has chosen to make a clean break from her past."

Queenie's frown got deeper as they stepped off the sand and onto sandstone. She silently stood as the Sheikh handed her a thick, fluffy white towel with gold Arabic letters emblazoned along the borders. "What does a clean break mean?" she asked even as the realization dawned on her. "Wait. Are you saying Renita is . . . she's gonna . . . she's planning to . . ."

"Yes," the Sheikh said, his eyes blazing green as he pulled on a black silk robe and looked down from his towering height. "She has announced that she will undergo an abortion in Europe. She is going to abort my child, Queenie. She is going to kill my baby."

17

Queenie stared at her drivers license. It said "State of Alaska" on it. She'd been staring at it for several minutes. Or perhaps it had been an hour. It was hard to say. She'd gone to her chambers and thought about packing, but then it had occurred to her that she didn't have any things because she'd been brought here in the middle of the night, a Christmas present for the Sheikh of Wakhrani. She also didn't have a passport, which meant it would be kinda hard to get back into the United States. It was kinda random that she had her drivers license, but she'd stuck it in her jeans that night so she'd remember to apply for a Texas license before the new year. The drivers license would probably be enough to establish her identity, and then they'd put her in a holding cell while Homeland Security verified that she wasn't an American jihadist returning from the Middle East after attending Terrorist Training Camp. It would be painful, but eventually they'd let her into the country, right?

"Right, but maybe they'll escort me from that holding cell at the airport directly to a holding cell in Juno State Penitentiary," she muttered, her mind swirling as she wondered if Homeland Security would investigate her background thoroughly enough to notice that she'd been linked to at least three different fires in Juno. No proof, but sometimes a pattern itself is proof! And then she'd have to explain how the hell she got to the Middle East with no money or a passport!

"You could just tell them the damned truth," she said to herself out loud. But then she laughed, shaking her head when she realized the truth was ridiculous. Besides, did she really want to stand there and claim she'd been kidnapped and transported across international borders by a devious Sheikh with green eyes and rock-hard . . . abs? What happens when they ask around and find out about the kiss beneath the mistletoe? Shit, there was probably video of that kiss! Security footage at the office—not to mention like fifty iPhone cameras recording it in high-definition!

"Or you could just stay here," she finally said, turning towards a full-length mirror with a hand-carved teakwood frame. "You said you're in this to win this, right? Then you need to stay here. Face the situation. Fight for what you want, for what's right!"

But what was right in this situation, Queenie wondered. What did Bawaar want? She wasn't worried that he'd want to get back with Renita, no matter what tricks the bitch pulled. Losing the child, however, would have an impact on him—that much she could tell. He hadn't seemed particularly thrilled by the prospect of Renita giving birth to his heir—or whatever the kid would be depending on the laws—but clearly the thought of her aborting the child didn't sit well with him.

"What to do?" she whispered, absentmindedly flipping her drivers license over and looking down at it. An image of that green car came floating back to her, and along with it the sickening memory of that blue-eyed driver, that man who'd lied to her, tricked her, shown her that she was a home-wrecker and a whore. Was that happening again? Should she walk away from this? After all, it was a family situation, wasn't it? Private. Between Bawaar and Renita. They'd been married over a decade! Yeah, they'd gotten divorced before Queenie had arrived on the scene, but certainly there were complexities here she couldn't possibly understand. Was she once again inserting her bit butt between a man and his family? Should she step aside and let them sort it out on their own, resolve it as a family matter?

That's for him to decide, not you, came the answer

from somewhere inside her, the part of her that wanted to hold on to this, to him, to that vision of the future. It made her feel sick again. Was she a gold-digger? She couldn't possibly be in "love" with Bawaar, could she?

"Whatever," she said, shaking her head. "The only time you actually believed you were in love, it ended in disaster. So it's better if you decide that you're a gold-digger or whatever and just embrace it. There's a reason you used to get lost in those romance novels as a teenager. There's a reason millions of women obsessively read those same books. It's because that kind of fairy-tale love doesn't exist. Things don't work out that way in real life. Billionaire kings don't fall in love with cleaning ladies. There's always a catch. Always a twist. And chances are it's the cleaning lady who's getting played."

"Why are you playing with your hair like that?" came the Sheikh's deep voice from behind her, and Queenie almost jumped out of her skin.

"How long have you been standing there?" she asked, turning red when she realized she'd been talking out loud, turning her open hair into knots to match how her insides were twisting up.

"Long enough," said the Sheikh coming close and sliding his arm around her waist. "Listen, Queenie. This thing with Renita . . ."

"You don't need to say anything," Queenie said

firmly, looking down at his arm and then up into his eyes. "I understand. You need to sort it out, and I'm just a complication. It's none of my business."

The Sheikh frowned, a flash of anger passing across his handsome face. He shook his head. "Of course it is your business," he said. "We are to be married. *She* is the complication, not you!"

Queenie closed her eyes and tried to fight back the feeling that she was in over her head, that this was a world of kings and queens, money and power, and she had no clue what everyone's motives were. Yeah, the chemistry between the Sheikh and her was real—she'd been with enough men to know what a real physical connection felt like, how rare it was, how special it was.

"So what do you want to do?" she asked stubbornly. "Get married and ignore the fact that your ex-wife is pregnant with your child and is now threatening to have an abortion?"

The Sheikh took a breath. "Yes. I will ignore it. It is Renita's choice, so let her make it. If she is bluffing just to get a reaction out of me, then we will call her bluff, see if she will go through with it. But—"

"But what if she's not bluffing? What about your reaction if she does actually go through with it? How would you feel if she does actually abort your child?"

"How would *you* feel about it?" the Sheikh said, blinking and drawing back from her, his green eyes narrowed in a way that told Queenie he was shutting himself off from Renita, from the situation.

"Don't make this about me," she snapped. "I'm not your escape route. I won't be responsible for you turning your back on your . . . your *family*!"

"Renita is *not* my family!" the Sheikh thundered, reaching for her hand as Queenie stepped back, finding herself flush against the floor-standing mirror. "Anyway, both Renita and family have brought me nothing but pain, done nothing but restrict my freedom, forced me to make choices I did not want to make!"

"Then you should have refused to marry Renita in the first place," Queenie said, her jaw tightening as the fight rose up in her. She wasn't going to be a crutch for Bawaar. She wasn't going to be an excuse for him to avoid choices that he had to make. "It's too late to change the past. And denying the past doesn't change a thing either. Be a man and face your choices."

The Sheikh's body tensed up as Queenie spoke, and as he clenched his fists she felt a flash of fear pass through her. But then he just smiled, taking control of himself and his anger.

"You dare talk to me about denying the past?" He shrugged. "Though I suppose you are qualified to do so."

"What do you mean?" she asked, her breath catching in her throat.

"I am not a fool," said the Sheikh. "You think I am so enamored by your beauty and charm that I decided to marry you without looking into your past?"

Queenie stared at the Sheikh dumbstruck. Had she really believed that? God, she was a moron, wasn't she? This man was the leader of a kingdom! He had security services and spies at his disposal! One phone call and he could probably get a file on her so detailed that he'd know when she first got her period!

"Well," she said, swallowing hard as she tried to stay calm. "If you know everything about my past and are still willing to marry me, then maybe you *are* enamored by my beauty and charm. Not to mention my wit."

As she said the words a calmness spread throughout her body, and Queenie realized that what she'd said was true, wasn't it? If he knew about her past with men, her past with the fires, her less-than-honorable deeds . . . yeah, if he knew all that and he was still here, didn't it mean this was real, this was true, this was . . . forever?

But doubt was knocking on the door again, and Queenie began to second-guess herself once more as she watched the Sheikh blink and shrug. Was he bluffing? Was he lying? Was he still playing her? Was she a patsy, brought into this drama for a purpose that had nothing to do with her beauty, charm, or wit?

"No," she said before the Sheikh could respond.

"I'm in over my head here. I know it. I feel it. I need to distance myself from this until you sort out whatever you need to with Renita and the baby and all that. I can't be involved with it. If you figure it out and you're still single, you know where to find me."

The Sheikh straightened up, his eyes going wide with surprise. He opened his mouth, but then clamped his jaw tight before saying a word. "You are fired," he said softly, looking directly into her eyes.

Queenie frowned and cocked her head to the left. "Excuse me?"

"You are fired," he said again. "Your employment has been terminated, effective immediately. I am still your boss, remember?"

Queenie snorted in disbelief. "Are you being serious? Fired for what?"

The Sheikh folded his arms across his chest and shrugged. "I do not need a reason to fire an employee."

"You are the most unbelievably immature, ridiculously impulsive, freak of a human being! You're seriously firing me because I refused to marry you?! And I haven't actually refused, by the way. I just said you need to figure this stuff out on your own, and then we'll see if there's anything here."

"If the answer is not yes, then it is no," said the Sheikh, arms still folded, eyes still narrowed. "And in fact the proposal has been withdrawn. If I cannot trust you to stand by my side when there is a crisis, what use are you?"

"What *use* am I? Is that what a wife is supposed to be? Someone to be *used*?!" Queenie was yelling and she had no idea why, but damn it felt good!

"Do not put words into my mouth!" the Sheikh responded, his own voice rising.

Queenie just raised her arms and shook her head, not sure whether to laugh or just keep yelling. "All right. I'm done here. You're obviously just an overgrown teenager with too much money, too much power, and too little of a grasp on reality. Forget what I said about finding me if you sort things out with Renita. I'm done. I'm gone. Also, I quit."

"You will quit when I say you can quit," the Sheikh said.

"You just fired me, you moron," she snapped. "Now, since you kidnapped me and I don't have a phone, money, or a passport, please transport me back to the United States the same way you brought me here."

The Sheikh took a long, deep breath, his gaze moving up and down along her body as Queenie shifted uncomfortably on her bare feet. Her hair was open, and she had no underwear on beneath her long white gown. Suddenly she felt vulnerable even as she sensed her nipples tightening, her vagina slowly secreting a wetness that made her clamp her buttcheeks together. She couldn't interpret the look he was giving her, nor could she understand her body's reaction. She wanted to be disgusted and angry with him, not turned on!

"I will send you back to America," he whispered, taking a step towards her as he undid his thick leather belt, "but not without your Christmas present. That would be rude, yes?"

Queenie blinked as she tried to back up. But she was already against the heavy mirror, and she pressed her ass against the cool glass as her heat rose. "What are you talking about?"

"If you decide you want nothing to do with me again, then so be it. But you will carry my child," he said. "You want to distance yourself from the Renita drama? Fine. But I will put you in the same position. Get you pregnant. Let us see what you do, yes? Perhaps you are already pregnant from when we made love on Christmas Day. But if not, I will make sure of it by putting my seed in you a third time. Come. Down on the carpet, my queen. Spread for me. Spread for your king."

18

"Spread for your king," the Sheikh heard himself say as he slipped his leather belt out from the loops of his tailored trousers. The blood was pounding in his temples, his erection pitching a violent peak. His mind was a mess as he thought of Renita and what she was doing. And now Queenie was turning her back on him! Ya Allah, throughout his life women had pushed and pulled him, twisted and turned him. His four mothers! Renita! And now Queenie!

No more, he decided as he took in the sight of Queenie pressed up against the mirror, her nipples clearly visible through her white gown. He glanced down along her curves, his breath catching when he saw the outline of her dark triangle through the sheer cloth. Ya Allah, she had no panties on! She was dripping for him!

"To hell with you," she said, taking a step forward and trying to push past him.

But the Sheikh grabbed her arms and pushed her back against the mirror, slamming her against the glass, which shuddered and shook but did not break. "I am already in hell," he muttered. "How else can you explain my life? How else can you explain these demons dressed as women who have tormented me, kept me from doing as I please, to whomever I please?! I am a *king*, by Allah! No one, especially not the women in my life, tells me what to do!"

Queenie's eyes went wide and she snorted. "You misogynistic pig! So you're blaming your mothers and your ex-wife and now me for everything you don't like in your life? Have you ever considered that maybe you're just a pig with a deep-rooted hatred of women?"

"Hate comes from somewhere, does it not? It is a reaction to something. To someone," the Sheikh said, holding her wrists above her head and leaning in as he spoke.

"Yeah, a reaction to *you*!" she said, almost spitting into his face as her mouth twisted. "You hate *yourself*, Bawaar! You hate yourself for allowing your mothers to bully you into marrying a woman you didn't love.

Mistletoe for the Sheikh

You hate yourself for staying in the marriage for so long. And now you hate yourself for not having the strength to deal with the situation on your own."

The Sheikh grinned, madness clawing at his insides as he breathed deep of Queenie's scent. She was freshly bathed, no makeup on, no perfume or deodorant. He could smell her natural musk from her bare armpits as he held her arms up. As he breathed deeper he picked up the tangy aroma of her cunt from beneath her loose gown. He was so hard now he could barely see, and he leaned in and kissed her hard on the mouth as she tried to turn her head away.

"What the fuck are you doing?" she said. "Are you insane?"

"You insult me. You tease me. You call me a coward. You call me weak. You are no different from every other woman in my life," he growled as he tightened his grip on her wrists and kissed her again. "Well, if this is the kind of woman I am destined to be with, then I will accept it. And so will you."

"You're not fit to be with *any* woman!" Queenie said. "You're a misogynistic nutcase from the goddamn stone age! Now let me go, or—"

"Or what?" he whispered, licking her neck as she shuddered and closed her eyes as if she was trying to fight the arousal that he could feel rising up in her. "Or you will scream? Fight? Cry like a little girl? Go on. Do what you will. If I am a woman-hating monster, then why would I care?"

Queenie turned her head and snapped her teeth at him like an animal, taking the Sheikh by surprise and getting him square on the nose. He roared in shock, feeling her teeth break the skin as tears welled up in his eyes and blood rolled down from the bridge of his nose.

"Ya Allah!" he roared, laughing as he felt the pain sting him. "Who is the animal now?"

"I never called you an animal," she said, grinning like a madwoman, his blood on her lips. "Your hatred for women is too complex and deep-rooted."

"You keep saying I hate women," the Sheikh said, taking deep breaths as he tried to slow his heartrate and bring himself under control before he gave life to a part of himself he had repressed for too long—perhaps forever. "But I love you, Queenie."

"Hah!" she squealed, looking away and then back at him. "That's a good one!"

"And you love me too," he whispered. "You are in this, like it or not."

"I *don't* like it. Now unhand me."

"Unhand me?" the Sheikh said, chuckling as he tightened his grip on her wrists, slamming her against the mirror and making the old glass shudder once again. "Is that a line from *Mills & Boon*? I understand there is an entire subgenre of romance that deals with my kind, yes?"

"You mean misogynistic rapists? Yeah. Not my style though."

"You like calling me a misogynist, don't you? Such a fancy word. I suggest you stop reading *Cosmo*. It fills your silly little head with very big ideas."

Queenie stared at him like she was trying to figure out whether he was serious or not. The Sheikh grinned, and she couldn't help show her smile. Bawaar almost shouted out in joy, because now he could see it, he could feel it, he could damn well *taste* it. This was real. *They* were real. The chemistry was undeniable, and even though the situation was a holy mess, this one thing was clear: She was his, and he was going to take her.

And so he pulled her away from the mirror, and in one swift motion ripped that thin white gown off her, tearing it along the side seam as she screamed in shock, her brown eyes wide as she covered her breasts and backed away from him.

"I said it once, and I will say it again," he growled as he unzipped his trousers and dropped them, pulled off his shirt and tossed it across the room. He stretched his massive arms to the side, opening up his chest, feeling his joints crack in approval. He smiled when he saw her gaze move down along his bronzed, rock-hard body and then rest on the peaked front of his black silk underwear. "Spread for me. Spread for your king, Queenie. Do not make me say it a third time."

19

"Third time's a charm," she said, still covering her boobs as she sidestepped the Sheikh, trying to keep her gaze fixed on his eyes even though the sight of his heavy erection was extremely distracting.

She wasn't sure when this thing had turned from her spitting in his face and calling him a woman-hating loser to where they were both naked and circling each other like fighters in a ring. Nothing had been resolved. If anything, things were more of a mess than ever before. But one thing was clear: There was a connection here. Call it chemistry, destiny, instinct . . . whatever. It was there, and it was real.

Maybe this *is* destiny, she thought as he reached for her and she swatted away his hand, not sure if she was playing or serious. Maybe this time I don't get to run. Maybe this time I take what I want, I get what I want. Maybe this time I need to commit to see this through, no matter where it goes. And what better way to commit than by letting him do what he says, by getting me pregnant? Renita wants to use his child as a weapon? All right, bitch. I can play that same game. Bring it on.

He was on her just as she finished the thought, grabbing her by the hair and smothering her with ferocious kisses, slamming her against the wall and grinding his massive cock and balls against her mound until she moaned and spread her legs wide.

"Oh, *fuck!*" she moaned as she felt him reach between their bodies and spread her slit with his fingers, pushing his enormous cockhead into her opening almost immediately.

The Sheikh grunted as he bent his knees slightly and then drove upwards into her, sliding his shaft all the way deep, so goddamn deep her eyes rolled up in her head and the only sound she could make was a throaty, gurgling whimper as he began to fuck her with everything he had.

Queenie came once, twice, three times in quick succession, her orgasms riding in like waves of stampeding Arabian horses. The Sheikh's fingers were digging into her buttocks, his breathing heavy against her head and neck. She was held firm against the wall, her legs wrapped around his waist as he held her up and pounded her with a force that rattled her teeth, made her flesh tremble like a train was going through her insides.

Finally he came, his motion barely slowing down as he blasted his load up into the farthest reaches of her vagina, pumping with a desperation that seemed to fit with the madness of what was happening. She could feel his hot semen flood her from the insides, and she gasped and groaned as she felt herself fill up even as the Sheikh kept pushing more of his load into her as if he had an endless supply in those massive balls that she could feel swinging up against her underside.

"Ya Allah," he said, panting as he slowed down, pulled back, and then rammed back in and held himself there, squeezing out the final drops of his royal seed. "If that does not make a baby, nothing will."

Queenie was too spent to do much more than smile and then drop her head onto his shoulder. They stayed in that position, her legs wrapped around him, his cock still all the way inside her like they were inseparable, like they were one, joined in both body and spirit.

"I can't believe I let you do that," she groaned, slowly unwrapping her legs as she felt his cock begin to slide out of her. She leaned against his hard body as she found her footing, and then she looked up into his green eyes and shook her head. "I was just gonna go home, away from this madness. I just wanna go home."

"This is your home now," said the Sheikh. "I am your home."

Queenie closed her eyes and took a breath. "What about Renita? What about—"

"It is time to address the Renita situation face to face. But we will do it together. You and I. King and Queen."

Queenie opened her eyes and blinked. Immediately she saw that he wasn't just commanding her, but he was also asking. Truly asking. He needed her help. He needed her to stand by him. She was in it now, all the way in. This was her drama now, she knew. No more running away.

"All right," she said softly, nodding her head. "All right. When?"

The Sheikh raised an eyebrow and looked at his watch, which was the only item of clothing on his naked body. He looked remarkably elegant despite his cock hanging down and still dripping all over the hand-woven Persian rug.

"She should be landing in about thirty minutes. Enough time for us to get ready, yes?"

Queenie frowned. "She's on her way here from Europe? You just invited her to come discuss this and she said yes?"

The Sheikh shrugged as he reached for his trousers. "Invited is a strong word. It is perhaps not the word Renita would use."

"Wait, so you kidnapped her?"

Bawaar shrugged again. "Kidnapped is a strong word too. But it is perhaps the word she will use when we meet with her."

Queenie shook her head and took a breath. "What about her European bodyguards?"

The Sheikh grinned. "No Europeans were harmed, I assure you, my queen. Anders Van Hosen will be accompanying my ex-wife, doing what he is paid to do." He paused and then shrugged for the third time. "Of course, now he is being paid by me, not Renita."

Queenie couldn't help but laugh. "So you bought out Anders Van Hosen, and paid him to kidnap his own client. I actually thought they were together when they showed up at the Christmas party."

Bawaar shook his head. "I am certain she paid him to make it appear that way. Van Hosen is a professional. He would never sleep with a client."

Queenie went quiet for a moment. "Does she want you back?" she said softly. She knew the answer, but she needed to ask the question. She had to know what she was dealing with when she faced Renita.

"I do not think even Renita knows what she wants,"

said the Sheikh without a moment's hesitation. "It is possible she does, in the same way a child wants something only when it is taken away. Perhaps she has decided that life as a common European billionairess is not as exciting as it sounds."

"So you think she wants her Palace and her throne and her title back? And the pregnancy drama is all made up? Seems pretty extreme. Especially if she isn't actually pregnant, right? I mean, there's only so long she can pretend to be pregnant if she's faking it!" Queenie blinked and took a breath. "When did you say you last fucked her?"

She didn't mean for her tone to be so flippant, and when Queenie heard herself almost spit out the last line, she knew she needed to be careful. It wasn't like Queenie was some model of self-control or self-awareness. She had her own issues, and she knew they were simmering beneath the surface.

"Two months ago," Bawaar said, frowning as he glanced into her eyes. He hesitated like he was going to say something more, but then clearly thought better of it and kept his mouth shut.

Queenie thought about it for a moment. She'd seen Renita a few days earlier at the Christmas party, and the woman looked slim like a rail. Two months pregnant? It was still possible. Some women didn't show until later. What the hell was this woman's game?!

"Well," Queenie said, brushing away the thought of the Sheikh having sex with that woman. She hated herself for that trace of jealousy, that annoying feeling of "Stay away from my man, bitch!" But then she just shrugged and accepted it. So what, she told herself. No shame in being protective. And anyway, this is your issue, not his. He's been clear that he wants nothing to do with his ex-wife, doesn't love her, isn't attracted to her, and is even willing to turn his back on his unborn child for you. If you're still jealous, it's your issue, not his!

"Well what?" said Bawaar, his jaw tightening in a way that Queenie could tell was because of stress. "Are you in this with me, or do I need to worry about you losing your cool when Renita walks in here with Van Hosen and a perfectly scripted piece of melodrama?"

"I'll be cool," Queenie said, closing her eyes and nodding slowly. She could feel an energy building up in her, and for a moment she didn't understand what it was. Then she got it. It was a feeling of power. Confidence. Coolness. She was going to stand by his side, act like a queen, and finish this story her fucking way. She'd been born an unwanted child, grown up a slutty teenager, and become a cleaning lady in Texas. Well, so what? Now she was about to be a queen, and that was how her story was gonna end. It was all in her hands. All she had to do was act like a queen!

Fake it till you make it.
In it to win it.
Bring it, you bitch. Let's see what you got.

20

"You did not bring her? Where is Renita?" thundered the Sheikh, taking a step towards the tall, blonde Anders Van Hosen.

The Austrian stood his ground, his blue eyes cool and unblinking, his clean-shaven jaw square and tight. Queenie stared at the two men facing off, wondering what the hell was going on. Van Hosen had walked in alone, escorted by the Sheikh's guards. Although he was calm, Queenie could sense a vague smugness in his expression.

"I run a security agency," he said smoothly, his gaze fixed on the Sheikh. "My reputation is everything.

How long do you think I would stay in business if I sold my clients out to the highest bidder?"

The Sheikh took a breath and shifted on his feet. Then he smiled, and Queenie frowned as it occurred to her that Bawaar did not look particularly shocked. He was angry, yes. But not surprised.

"Fair enough," said the Sheikh. "So then why are you here? Why not just refuse me? You needed the money? Is that it? Security business in a slump? The Van Hosen portfolio has taken a beating in the stock market? Speak up."

"I had my bankers decline the wire transfer. The money is back in your accounts. It is blood money."

"Very honorable. I will make sure I recommend you to anyone who asks. Now answer my question: Why bother to show up here, Anders? Clearly this is part of Renita's game." The Sheikh smiled and shook his head, his green eyes narrowing. "Or do you not see that yet? Has she got you dancing to her tune as well, Anders Van Hosen? The Austrian Waltz? Hah!"

Van Hosen finally blinked, and Queenie saw a shadow of doubt pass across his face. "Ms. Renita has taken ill," he said softly. "She was planning to accompany me here, even though I told her everything. She wanted to meet with you face to face." For the first time Van Hosen turned his head and glanced at Queenie. "She wanted to meet with both of you. Come to an agreement. End this once and for all."

"Ill?" said the Sheikh, raising an eyebrow and rubbing his chin. "Renita has called in sick to the finale of her own drama? Stage fright?"

"A complication with the pregnancy," said Anders. "It could be serious."

The Sheikh blinked, and Queenie saw him draw a sharp breath. "Where is she?" he asked.

"Safe. Stable," said Van Hosen. He looked down at a slim leather attaché he'd been carrying, and then glanced up at the Sheikh. "May I?" he said.

The Sheikh looked at his two guards, and they both nodded. "Go on," said Bawaar.

"Here is Renita's proposal," Van Hosen said, opening the case and pulling out a single sheet of thick, cream-colored paper. "She asked me to deliver it."

The Sheikh snatched the paper from Van Hosen's hand, his gaze lingering on the Austrian before he glanced quickly at Queenie and then down at the page. Queenie watched Bawaar's face change color as he read, and then he shook his head and handed the paper to Queenie.

"This is ridiculous," he said softly. "I should behead you and send my men to every hospital in Vienna until they find that witch. Then I should behead her, and bury all three of you together, that abomination of a child included."

Queenie frowned as she read the options Renita had presented, and she felt the blood drain from her cheeks when she got to the end:

"If you don't agree, I will kill myself and the baby,

making sure I release a recorded video suicide note detailing that Queenie Quinn, Alaskan home-wrecker, is the reason I chose to end two lives."

Queenie staggered back as she read her own name on the paper. What the hell?! When did this become about her? Yeah, there'd been that public kiss beneath the mistletoe, but that was just a few days ago. No way Renita would know that Bawaar and Queenie were . . . were *together*! She stared up at the Austrian before looking back down at the paper. The options were clearly laid out:

Option 1: Void our divorce and take me as your first wife and Sheikha. We will have our child, and the child will be heir of Wakhrani. You may still marry Queenie Quinn, but she will be the Second Wife, always and forever. I will agree to allow the laws to be changed back to the old tradition where a Sheikh is allowed multiple wives. By day you will hold court with me by your side, and by night you can take her like the whore she is, satisfy the animalistic urges that I am too much of a lady to entertain.

Option 2: We stay divorced, and you can do as you please with Queenie Quinn except marry her or have children with her. You may take other wives over the course of your life, but never will you marry Queenie Quinn, and never will she bear your child. Our child will be born, and will be the heir of Wakhrani according to the laws of the first-born ascendancy.

She read past the strange ultimatum of the suicide,

shaking her head again as she tried to figure out what the hell was happening. Why did Renita hate Queenie so much? Was it just misdirected hatred for the Sheikh? Did she just want to hurt Bawaar, and so had decided the best way was to humiliate both the Sheikh and Queenie by denying them the chance to be truly together as man and wife? How could this make any sense?!

"I don't get it," Queenie said, biting her lip as she read the note again. Her gaze stopped on the word "Alaskan," and she frowned and stared. Renita had called her an Alaskan whore, not an American one. Sure, it wouldn't have been hard to find out where Queenie was from; but still, it seemed odd.

Queenie blinked as she looked up at Anders Van Hosen. "Earlier you said Renita wanted to meet face-to-face with not just the Sheikh but me as well. How did she know I was here in Wakhrani? Were your people spying on me in America? Watching the Sheikh's Palace in Wakhrani?"

Bawaar whipped his head towards Van Hosen, his fists clenching as his eyes widened. "You dared spy on me in my own kingdom?! That is a violation, and you know it! How can you talk about reputation when you violate the basic rules of the business! I never threatened Renita, and you had no grounds to send your agency's people within my borders! Ya Allah, Van Hosen, I swear I will—"

"No!" said Van Hosen, and he closed his eyes tight

and shook his head, his white face turning red. "No," he said again, lowering his voice and shaking his head even harder. "I should never have taken this job," he began to mutter. "This is not going to end well for me or my family business. Our bread and butter is the political and corporate security businesses. This job is a family matter, and clearly I am not cut out for the level of insanity! At least in the political or business world, the motives and clear and logical. Money. Power. So simple. Easy to understand. But this . . . by God, this is beyond my capacity to understand! Why all you people will go to these lengths to hurt one another when there is neither money nor power at stake?!"

"Of course there is money and power at stake," said the Sheikh, fists still clenched. "Renita wants the throne back, and she wants her child to rule when I am dead! If that is not about power and money, then what is!"

Van Hosen took a deep breath, lowering his head and rubbing his eyes. "Clearly you do not know your own wife. Yes, she cares about money. But she is a billionairess after the divorce settlement, and she would be rich anyway just from her own Jordanian family inheritances. The money isn't a factor. As for power . . . yes, in a sense it is about power. But not political power. For them it's about power over individuals, power over your lives, power over . . . her."

He glanced at Queenie as he said *her*, and once again Queenie felt the blood rush from her face as she took a step back. But for some reason another word stuck in her mind:

"Them," she said, her head still spinning. "You said *them*, not *her*. You said 'For *them* it's about power over me.' But it's just Renita, isn't it? Or is there someone else involved?"

Van Hosen's face turned a sickly white, and for a moment it looked like he might pass out on his feet. He might have been very good at handling the most dangerous political situations, but clearly he was out of his league when it came to family drama. Queenie almost felt sorry for him when she realized he'd let something slip, said more than he was supposed to, revealed more than he'd planned.

"To hell with it," he muttered. "He would have revealed himself anyway. The plan was always for you to know. He would want you to know it was him."

"Who?" Queenie whispered, her own fists clenching as she took a step forward like she was prepared to beat it out of this European if she had to. "You better start talking, Van Hosen, or else we'll take you down to the dungeons and introduce you to some medieval-ass interrogation techniques that will make you scream for Mommy."

Queenie caught the Sheikh turn to her, his mouth twisting like he was trying to stop himself from laughing. She almost burst into a smile herself when she realized what she'd said with supreme confidence and conviction, like she was some evil queen from a fairy tale. But that chill was still running through her, and when Van Hosen finally took a breath and looked her square in the face, she staggered once again.

"The man whose family you destroyed back in Alaska," said Van Hosen. "He contacted Renita on Christmas morning. He told her you were here in Wakhrani, with the Sheikh. He told her everything."

Queenie's mouth hung open, but she couldn't speak for several long moments. "The man whose family I . . . destroyed?! In Alaska?!" She frowned as she thought back to that blue-eyed man with the green car, but that made no sense. It was so long ago! Over a decade ago! She was still nineteen then! No way!

Her mind spun as she tried to make sense of it all. The last she'd heard of Mister Blue-Eyes was when Mama said he'd shown up at the house looking for her. Mama had told him she was gone, whatever that meant. And then there was the fire, and Mama's death, and Queenie had moved to an apartment on the far side of town. Blue-Eyes was mostly forgotten in all that chaos, even though there'd been moments when Queenie had thought about him: sometimes hating him for lying to her; other times wondering what would have happened if she'd just said to hell with it, that she didn't give a shit that he had a family, that it was his choice to leave them for her, that he had a right to be happy and so did she. But he'd never contacted her again, and she'd let it go. At the end of it she knew she wasn't that woman, that she couldn't be the reason a man left his wife and children, no matter how he made her feel.

So why the hell would Blue-Eyes suddenly show up now, a decade later, talking to Renita about stuff Queenie had supposedly done back in Alaska?

There was only one explanation that made any sense:

Blue-Eyes wasn't suddenly showing up.

Blue-Eyes had never left.

Queenie blinked as her vision clouded, but her mind was clear as a bell. She could clearly think back to the first time Blue-Eyes had talked to her: It had been months after he'd been driving his green car to her gas station. So for months he'd seen her, maybe watched her in the rearview mirror, perhaps sat in his car and gazed at her as she handled the cash register inside the station. For months he'd just stayed in the shadows before coming forward with that story of the lottery and the offer to give her a car. She'd been a kid. She hadn't noticed the pattern back then, but it was clear now. Could it be that he'd kept his eye on her for a decade since then, waiting for a chance to . . . what, get revenge? Destroy her chance at being happy, at starting a family, at being someone's wife, a mother to someone's children? If he'd been watching her, then he'd have seen her getting kidnapped. Perhaps he'd followed her captors to the airport, watched the private jet painted with the Sheikh of Wakhrani's insignia take off from Juno's tiny airport.

And then he'd contacted Renita, someone who shared his obsession with making an ex-lover suffer when instead they should have been blaming themselves. What did he tell her? How did he convince her to issue that crazy list of options, ending with a threat to kill herself and the child just for . . . what, more revenge? To avenge the insult of the Sheikh taking another woman so soon? Who were these people! Who thinks like that?! Who *acts* like that!

Queenie glanced over at the Sheikh as her thoughts drifted to Renita. We're all in this together in a way that seems so crazy, but also makes complete sense, doesn't it? It was our own choices that brought these people into our lives, our own choices that kept them in our lives. Yeah, I was nineteen and vulnerable, swept off my feet by a sophisticated older man who wanted to give me gifts, hold my hand, and love me like I was a real woman. But I should have guessed it was too good to be true. Or perhaps I suspected it was too good to be true but didn't care. Didn't wanna know. Hell, perhaps I *am* that woman who doesn't give a damn who she steps on to get to her happily-ever-after!

Queenie blinked and swallowed as that last thought stuck in her throat like it was a fish-bone. Was she that woman? Ruthless, selfish, obsessed with her own happiness without regard for anyone else's?

"Oh, God, Bawaar," she whispered, turning to the Sheikh, only now realizing he'd been calmly looking at her for the past several minutes. "Oh, God, I'm a horrible person. I deserve this, don't I? I brought this on myself. On all of us!"

The Sheikh frowned, glancing quickly at Van Hosen and then back at Queenie. "Stop talking like you are as insane as the rest of these fools. None of this happens without Renita. It started with her, with her twisted, convoluted mind, her unrealistic sense of what matters. To her it is all about perception, what the world thinks of her. She is built up by compliments, broken by insults. And she sees you as an insult, a threat to her self-image. That is why she is lashing out in such an inexplicably personal way even though she does not know you."

Queenie shook her head, biting her lip as she thought back to Blue-Eyes. She felt a shiver make its way through her body like a dark wave as she remembered how that green car had driven up to the gas station every two days like clockwork, always on her shift. Had she been secretly turned on by the thought of having a stalker, a man obsessed with her, a man prepared to walk away from his wife and kids for her? She wasn't sure if she was sickened by Blue-Eyes or herself!

Once again she looked at the Sheikh, her toes curling up as if prompting her to run. She glanced toward the door, the absurd thought of physically running away from this crossing her mind. But of course there was nowhere to run. No one to run to.

"Where is she?" the Sheikh said, turning to Van Hosen, his voice like cold steel. "Is this illness real or manufactured? It is time to talk, Van Hosen. This is not your game, and you know it. You want to save your reputation, keep your family business clean enough that future clients will trust you, then it's time for you to step out of the way. Where is she?"

Van Hosen glanced at the two guards flanking him, and then he slowly shook his head. "The sooner I get back to the safety of political assassinations and corporate kidnappings the better," he muttered. "All right, Sheikh. You win. You win. You all deserve each other. I am bowing out."

21
__SOMEWHERE IN EUROPE__

"**S**hould I bow when I enter her presence?" Queenie asked as their limousine pulled up to the address Van Hosen had given them.

It was a small town somewhere between France and Germany, and the Sheikh had grunted in recognition when he'd seen the address.

"One of the properties I gave her in the divorce," he'd said on the flight over. "I did not even remember I owned this place."

Queenie had shaken her head and smiled. "Van Hosen was right. You guys are not normal people.

Who the hell has mansions in Europe that they just kinda forgot about?!"

The Sheikh had looked at her and smiled. "More people than you might think. But technically Renita owns it now. And no, you should not bow when in her presence. She is no longer royalty—at least not Wakhrani royalty—and she needs to be reminded of it."

"Is that wise? To insult her when this whole drama has been spun by her reaction to being insulted?"

"You want to just give in to her? All right then. Which option do you choose? To be my second wife, sharing the Royal Palace with Renita, who will live out her days satisfied that you will always be beneath her in the hierarchy? Or perhaps you like Option Two, where you can live as my girlfriend or whore or one-woman harem. No wedding ring. No children."

Queenie laughed as the limousine stopped outside the gates of the mansion. "How about Option Three, where she just kills herself on Facebook Live while screaming your name. It'll be like the ending scene in *Braveheart*, where Mel Gibson dies a horrible death for the sake of principle. And we'll live happily ever after as the evil king and queen."

"That is a smashing idea. From now on I will base all my major decisions on the movies of Mel Gibson," said the Sheikh, raising an eyebrow as he pulled out his phone and tapped on it. He glanced up as the automated gates slowly swung open. "Ah, at least she did not change the code."

The limousine stopped outside the front door, and the Sheikh's guards stepped out from the car. They surveyed the area before knocking on the front door, and the Sheikh placed his hand on Queenie's as they waited.

No one answered the door, and finally the Sheikh got out of the car and simply pushed on the old brass handle. The door swung open, and the Sheikh's guards rushed in as Bawaar held his arm up, indicating that Queenie stay in the car until he gave the all-clear.

"Whatever," Queenie said, getting out of the car and walking up to the Sheikh as he sighed and shook his head. "What's she gonna do? Throw a pointy heel at me? Stab me with her hip-bone? If she wanted to physically hurt me, she would have had it done, don't you think?"

The Sheikh grunted as they waited for his guards to search the house. "Perhaps you understand Renita better than I ever did."

"Perhaps," said Queenie, and the Sheikh smiled when he noticed the seriousness in her tone. "But what bothers me is—"

She was cut off by one of the Sheikh's guards running down the main staircase, calling out in Arabic.

"Iidha kunt tatahadath alearabiat, aismahuu li 'an 'aerif," he said, his eyes wide.

The Sheikh frowned, and then he turned to Queenie. "Stay here," he commanded, glancing at one of his guards and nodding to make sure the guard stood by Queenie's side. Then the Sheikh bounded up the stairs, two steps at a time, until he was at the top.

"Ya Allah," he muttered when he saw the body on the floor. "What in God's name?!"

"Oh, God!" came her voice from behind him, and the Sheikh turned to see Queenie standing right there, her chest heaving from running up the stairs. Of course she'd disobeyed him.

"Is that him?" Bawaar asked, taking a breath as he glanced at the dead man. The man was older, with deep wrinkles that made his face look he was still thinking about something even in death.

Queenie nodded silently as one of the Sheikh's guards knelt over the dead man and checked his pulse before glancing up and shaking his head. "Why is he here?" she said softly. "Why is he . . . oh, God, Bawaar! What's happening? Why would Renita do that?"

"She would not," said the Sheikh, rubbing his jaw as he began to pace. "That is not her way. She would rather hurt herself in order to bring pain to others. Murder . . . ya Allah, no. It is not her style." He glanced up at Queenie, his eyes narrowing as he thought. "There is someone else involved, Queenie. Who?"

"His wife," said Queenie, blinking as she kept her gaze fixed on the dead man. "She tracked me down all those years ago. She must have been following him back then. Maybe she never stopped following him." She looked up and shook her head. "God, I don't even know if they stayed together back then. Don't even know if she'd still be his wife."

"Sounds like they deserve each other," the Sheikh muttered. "Everyone following everyone else, blaming someone else for their mistakes, exacting revenge instead of practicing forgiveness."

Queenie frowned. "Forgiveness? Who exactly are we going to forgive? And for what?"

"Ourselves," said the Sheikh without hesitating, even though he was as surprised at his words as Queenie appeared to be. "I have been blaming myself for turning Renita into this person, a caricature of a human whose entire self-image was built on public perception. And so when that was threatened, she broke, shattered, became unstable and unpredictable." He glanced at Queenie, reaching for her hand. She trembled when he touched her, and he knew she was affected by the sight of the dead man. Not just because it was a dead body, but also because the man had meant something to her. Not something good, necessarily—but he had played a role in her life, in making her the person she was. His queen.

She nodded as she tightened her grip on his hand. "And I've blamed myself for . . . for him. Even though he lied to me, lied to his wife, lied to his family . . . I still blamed myself a little. Maybe a lot. I don't know. Shit, I don't know, Bawaar."

The Sheikh took a breath and led Queenie from the room, glancing at one of his guards on the way out. The guard shook his head, indicating that the rest of the house was empty. Renita was gone.

"How did he die?" said Queenie when they walked down the stairs and sat side by side on a green velvet sofa facing a picture window. Outside were old trees, evergreens, with lush green branches laden with white snow. The Sheikh remembered planting one of those trees when he'd first bought the house, and he smiled as he felt a strange, almost fatherly pride at how tall and strong it had grown.

"There is no blood, so he was not shot or stabbed. Poison, perhaps? I do not know."

"We should call the police," said Queenie, her eyes going wide as if the thought of the police worried her.

The Sheikh smiled. "My guards will take care of things. There are other things for us to take care of."

"Like what?"

"Like ourselves. Are you all right, Queenie? I know . . . I mean, I understand that this man was a part of your past, played a role in turning you into the woman you are. The woman I love. So it is only natural to feel something. Grief. Or perhaps—"

"Relief," said Queenie firmly, looking him directly in the eyes so he could see she was serious as hell.

"Yes, he was a part of my life. Yes, whatever happened with him affected me in more ways than I probably understand. But I was nineteen the last time I saw him, Bawaar! I'm in my thirties now! If he'd been watching me all these years, waiting for a chance to . . . to get revenge for what he thinks I did to his life?! Shit, I'm glad he's dead! I'm sorry if that sounds cold, but to hell with him! I'm *glad* he's dead!"

The Sheikh put his arm around Queenie and pulled her into him, and then she broke. The sobs came hard and heavy, and the Sheikh cradled her like a child as she bawled into his chest.

"I don't even know why I'm crying!" she said, laughing and sputtering. "I really don't give a shit about him. You know that, don't you?"

"Yes. But it does not matter. Your past does not matter to me. You know that, do you not?"

Queenie sniffled as she took the silk handkerchief held out by the Sheikh. "I thought you investigated my past before deciding to marry me."

The Sheikh grunted and shrugged. "That was just to prove to you that your past does not matter. I knew that no matter what I learned about you, it would not change how I felt."

Bawaar felt her breathe deep beside him, and he pulled her even closer as he watched those trees sway silently outside the thick glass, drizzling snowflakes like it was all staged. It felt like he was watching a movie, a surreal play or drama. Slowly his mind was pulled back to the reality, which was more surreal than any movie he'd ever seen, more convoluted than even the Arabic epics he'd read in school.

"You know, it's possible that his wife isn't involved at all," Queenie said slowly, and the Sheikh smiled when he saw that his queen was focused and together after her cry. She'd broken for a moment, but just like that she was back together, strong and ready for whatever came next. "I mean, he could just as easily have dropped dead of a heart attack. Just a coincidence, for all we know. And then maybe Renita got scared and just took off, thinking she'd get in trouble or something."

The Sheikh frowned as he pulled out his phone. "I cannot agree with the first part of that. But the rest of it is possible. Van Hosen's men would have been here all the while. So it is not like this wife could have kidnapped her or anything. Not unless she stormed in here with an army."

"An army of Eskimos? Unlikely," said Queenie, smiling and then raising her hand to her mouth. "Ohmygod, that's kinda racist, I think!"

"To use the word Eskimo is racist? Ya Allah! Next you will say that to call me an Arab is racist!"

Queenie shrugged. "Well, it does sound kinda racist when you say it in that tone."

"Now *that* is racist," declared the Sheikh, grinning as he felt a warm glow flowing through his body. Only now did it occur to him that it was still so early in their relationship, but already it felt like they were bound together, in this together . . . whatever this was.

This experience itself is a Christmas Gift, a Ramadan Miracle, a gift from the Gods, all of whom love this time of year, the Sheikh thought as he kissed her hair and watched the evergreens dust the landscape with snow as the breeze whispered through the branches. "There is a lesson in this experience," he said softly, his thoughts seamlessly flowing into speech. "A meaning that will define the rest of our relationship. A Christmas Gift that we will carry with us the rest of our lives."

Queenie giggled. "You sound like the narrator in some cheesy Christmas movie."

"You are mocking my Christmas spirit?

"Aren't you a Muslim?" Queenie said, frowning as she leaned away from him so she could see his expression.

"Yes, but Christianity and Islam have common origins. And this time of year is holy for Muslims as well. Besides, Christmas is about more than religion. Every nation and culture celebrates some version of Christmas. And because it is so close to the New Year, this is always a time of reflection, a time for new beginnings, a time for—"

"Sheikh," came his attendant's hesitant voice from behind him. "There is a phone call."

Bawaar took a breath, annoyed at first for the interruption. But then he looked at the phone in his hand and remembered that he'd meant to call Van Hosen anyway. It was probably Van Hosen calling him with word on Renita's whereabouts. Good. Time to finish this.

"Speak, Van Hosen," said the Sheikh into the golden iPhone the attendant offered. He leaned back and sighed again, but then immediately sat up straight when he heard the voice. "What?" he said, frowning as he listened. "Where did they drop her off?"

"What? Where is she?" Queenie said, grabbing his arm and leaning in.

The Sheikh flipped on the speaker so she could hear.

"Alaska?" said Queenie. "Did he just say the word Alaska?"

The Sheikh listened, and then turned to Queenie, his eyes as wide as hers as the trees outside began to sway violently in a sudden gust of wind. "Yes," he said slowly as his mind raced to put the pieces together. "He did indeed say Alaska."

22
__SOMEWHERE IN ALASKA__

"**I** don't get it," said Queenie, squinting as she took a left turn, heading directly into the sun.

"Me neither," said the Sheikh, putting on his sunglasses and looking at his watch. "According to my custom-made Rolex, it is almost midnight. But I could swear that yellow fireball directly ahead is the sun. Yes?"

Queenie snorted, glancing over at Bawaar and then back at the empty highway. There was really no good reason for them to even be here. But then again, there didn't seem to be a good reason for Renita to be here either. Perhaps that was why both she and the Sheikh had agreed to follow this through to the end. Rather than drive off into the sunset, they were now . . . well, still driving off into the sunset, it seemed.

"You know this is the Land of the Midnight Sun, right?" she said, fumbling around for her sunglasses and then cursing when she remembered she'd left them on the Sheikh's jet. "Goddamn it! I'm gonna have wrinkles from squinting so much! Can I borrow your sunglasses?"

"Absolutely not," said the Sheikh, pushing his shades back up on his nose and settling into the passenger-side seat of the Range Rover he'd purchased in cash from the dealership outside Anchorage just because he didn't like the selection of rental cars at the airport. "I am the face of a kingdom. It would not do for me to have wrinkles. Besides, I am not used to this midnight sun tomfoolery. I might get blinded. You would not want a blind husband, would you?"

Queenie shrugged, smiling as she relaxed in her seat and listened to the heavy car purr its way down the smooth highway as her fiancé's deep voice entertained her. *This feels like a honeymoon*, she thought. *Like a vacation. Like it doesn't matter why we're here, because it's just . . . fun!* "A blind husband wouldn't be so bad. That way I could just let myself go and you wouldn't notice. I'd be like nine hundred pounds by the time I'm forty. Bags under my eyes from binge-watching Netflix all day. Rolls of fat all over my body."

The Sheikh slid his hand over her belly and then placed it against the front of her jeans as she gasped and swerved before getting control of the car again.

"Go on," murmured the Sheikh as he rubbed her mound through her tight black stretch jeans. "You are only turning me on, woman. A hefty queen only exudes power and authority. Tell me again about you being nine hundred pounds of woman, with nipples the size of dinner plates. Let me see."

"See what?" Queenie said, swatting away his hand as he reached for the neckline of her pink sweater, pulling at it until she managed to stop him. "OK, this sweater doesn't open that way! You're gonna stretch it out of shape, you beast!"

"I want to stretch *you* out of shape. Stop the car," he growled, leaning over and kissing her neck as he reached across and grabbed her boob firmly, pressing so hard she almost honked the horn.

"Here?! Are you crazy!" she said, laughing as she arched her neck back and let the Sheikh massage her breast until she felt her nipple tighten beneath the soft lambswool. "Besides, we're on a mission, remember?"

The Sheikh sighed and pulled back, grunting as he turned his head away from her. "I suppose. All right. If you are so focused on your mission, then so be it. I will have to take matters into my own hands."

Queenie frowned as she saw the Sheikh recline his seat and fumble at his belt. Then she gasped in mock horror as he unzipped and pushed his wool pants down past his tight, muscular hips, sliding down his black silk underwear and releasing his mighty brown cock. It sprung up like the first shoots of spring, thick and heavy, its head dark red and swollen, and the Sheikh began to nonchalantly stroke himself as the midnight sun gazed down on them through the windshield.

"Oh. My. God," Queenie muttered, shaking her head in disbelief. "You are unbelievably sick. A total perv! Poor Renita! I can only imagine what she'd have done if you whipped out your cock like that!"

"Please do not mention her name or else I will lose my hardness," said the Sheikh. "Besides, what my ex-wife would have done is not relevant. The question is, what will *you* do, my queen?"

Queenie did her best to keep a straight face and focus on the road, but it was hard to ignore the massive pillar of a cock that was butting into the corners of her vision as the Sheikh shamelessly touched himself like a horny schoolboy. In a way it was sick, but it was also beautiful, natural, and utterly free of shame and self-consciousness. It was like he was opening up to her, showing himself in the light of the sun, not afraid to display every side of him: both his body and his personality. She'd made the comment about Renita without really thinking about it, but now it occurred to her how strange it was that she could mention his ex-wife's name like it was all just a running joke!

And in a way it *is* a big joke, isn't it, she thought as she finally smiled, shook her head, and then reached across the gearshift and grasped the Sheikh's cock as he groaned out loud, grinning wide and leaning back as she started to jerk him off, her eyes still on the road ahead.

Hell yeah, it's a big joke, she decided as she thought back to what they'd learned from Van Hosen's security people. Apparently they'd been asked to escort Renita safely to Alaska, USA, after which they'd been dismissed. Sent away. Relieved of their duties. Told they were no longer needed. It made no sense, Queenie had decided when she heard. It was too weird to be a coincidence. But it was too weird to be part of any coherent plan either! *Way* too weird!

It was only after the Sheikh had his own security services obtain footage from the cameras outside Anchorage International Airport that things made some sense . . . well, maybe not *sense*—more like a connection.

Queenie and the Sheikh had watched the airport footage, seen Renita dismiss Van Hosen's guards outside the private terminal for charter flights. She'd stood there alone at the curbside for several minutes, finally pulling out her phone and dialing. She'd said something, hung up, and waited a few more minutes. Then a ten-year-old white Ford Explorer had pulled up, and Renita had gotten in with a smile.

That was the only footage they had, and when the

Sheikh had his technicians freeze the picture and zoom in on the driver, Queenie had frowned when she saw that it was Blue-Eyes's wife. The same woman who'd showed up outside Mama's front door a decade earlier, calling nineteen-year-old Queenie a whore and a home-wrecker, threatening bloody murder as she screamed, "Get your own man, because this one is taken!"

"What the hell," Queenie had muttered, shaking her head in disbelief. "Are they like . . . *friends* now?!"

"Renita does not have any friends," the Sheikh had muttered, turning to his people and barking out orders in Arabic. "I will have my people pull up all information on this woman."

"Why?" said Queenie, not sure how she felt about what was happening. It was sickeningly confusing, the feeling that she was at the center of this somehow. "Just send the police there! She murdered her husband, didn't she? And Renita was part of the plan. Blue-Eyes was an American Citizen, and so Renita will be held in the United States until the trial is done. She can't have an abortion while in prison. And yeah, she could still kill herself, but I doubt she has the gumption to hang herself with a bedsheet or something!"

The Sheikh took a deep breath and turned to her. "My medical people examined Blue-Eyes," he said softly. "There is no evidence of foul play. No poison. No trauma—at least not any that was inflicted by someone else."

"What do you mean? So there was . . . self-inflicted trauma?"

"You could say that, I suppose. But no. My medical examiners reported that Blue-Eyes's insides were ravaged by cancer. Tumors eating away at every major organ." He'd waited a moment as Queenie took a breath, a shudder going through her as she tried to process all of it. "Also," said the Sheikh, his green eyes narrowing, "my examiners assure me that Blue-Eyes did not die in that room. He'd been dead for at least two days, his body kept cool and then transported to my house in Europe."

"Transported? From where?" Queenie had said, blinking and shaking her head.

Bawaar had shrugged at the time, but then they'd discovered Renita's whereabouts, seen the camera-footage, seen the driver of the white Ford Explorer.

"We can turn our backs on all this," the Sheikh had said to her, taking her hand. "Walk away from Renita's madness. I am prepared to do it. Let her do her worst. She wants to kill herself and her unborn child, so be it. I refuse to participate in her madness any longer. I want to move forward. Move forward with you. We are in no danger from her within the walls of the Royal Palace or anywhere we travel. She might as well not exist. She might as well be dead, in fact!"

Queenie had closed her eyes and taken several long breaths. Then she'd shaken her head and slowly opened her eyes. "The child is not just hers. It's yours too."

The Sheikh's jaw had tightened, and Queenie could see that he was trying to block out his own emotions. "I do not want the child," he'd said through gritted teeth, his gaze drifting down to the floor as if he didn't want to look into her eyes. "Neither does Renita. Perhaps it is better if she chooses to abort. After all, if the child is unwanted, it is better off not being born."

"The child isn't unwanted," Queenie had said, the words coming out before she even realized she was speaking. "I want the child."

The Sheikh's eyes had widened. "What are you talking about, Queenie? *You* want Renita's child?!"

"It's not just her child. It's yours too. And if we're going to be married, then in a way the child is mine also, right?" She'd shaken her head as her eyes welled with tears. "I was an unwanted child," she said softly. "Maybe I'm being tested here. Maybe the universe is offering me an unwanted child to see how I'll react, to see if I can . . . I don't know . . . forgive myself? Forgive my parents? Learn how my mother came to love an unwanted child? Learn how to love myself by finding it within me to love this child? After all, in all this we've only been thinking about ourselves, haven't we? Renita wants to hurt you by using her pregnancy to make you look bad in public. You want to fight her by turning your back on her drama and saying to hell with it, do what you want!"

"And what do *you* want?" the Sheikh had said, frowning and exhaling hard. "Do you not want to be with me? Build a life with me? Build your own family with me?"

"Of *course* I do! But I'm not going to let you turn your back on your own family so I can get what I want, Bawaar! You can have all of it. *We* can have all of it! We just need to open our hearts a little!" She'd paused as she remembered that all of this had started on Christmas Eve, manifested on Christmas Day. A time for love, forgiveness, and goodwill, wasn't it? A time for *family*!

"So what do you want to do, Queenie?"

"I want to go to her. Go to them both. Sit down and talk to them. Tell Blue-Eyes's wife that I never meant to hurt her or her family. Tell Renita that if she doesn't want the child, I'll love the kid like it's my own, raise it alongside my own babies, never stand in the way if the child eventually sits on the throne. That's the only way to finish it, Bawaar. We can't turn our backs. We can't run. We can't just burn it all down because we don't want to deal with it."

"I thought that was your way of dealing with things," the Sheikh had said, raising an eyebrow as a half-smile curled around the corner of his mouth. "Burn it down, run away, don't look back."

"I know," she'd said. "But it's Christmas, and New Years Day is around the corner. Time for forgiveness. Time for change. Time for new beginnings."

"All right then," the Sheikh had said softly, his green eyes bright with what Queenie could only interpret as love, perhaps with a hint of admiration, a glimmer of . . . relief? "Then I will try to find it in myself to forgive Renita too." He'd swallowed hard and taken a breath. "And I will admit that I do care about the child, that although there is no doubt in my mind that my future is with you, that you are my family, my queen, the to-be mother of my princes and princesses, I cannot turn my back on my past. I have to accept it, incorporate it, carry it with me."

"So then we're set," Queenie had said, trying to keep her voice from cracking as she felt the tears roll down her cheeks like ice melting. "We're heading north. To Alaska. Mush, baby!"

23

"**H**ave a Mushy Christmas!" she shouted, laughing out loud as they drove past a billboard showing a group of huskies pulling a sled with Santa Claus smiling down at them.

"Faster!" shouted the Sheikh, grasping her hand and tightening her grip on his cock as Queenie jerked him up and down. "Ya Allah, I am almost there! Mush! Mush!"

"You are ridiculous!" Queenie squealed, almost doubling over in laughter at the sight of the Sheikh, his pants down around his knees, cockhead bulging out the top of her fist which couldn't even close around his massive girth. And he was yelling *Mush* as she jerked him off as hard as she could! "*So* perverted!"

"I will show you perverted," the Sheikh growled, suddenly pulling her hand away from his cock, grabbing the steering wheel, yanking it sharply to the right, and heading straight for a gigantic snowbank along the shoulder of the road. "Hit the brakes, please."

Queenie screamed as the car smashed through the soft snow, drove off the road, and finally stopped about fifty yards away from the highway in a deep ditch. She'd slammed the brakes on in time so they didn't hit hard enough for the airbags to pop, but the car was leaning forward in the ditch, its rear wheels off the ground and spinning hopelessly.

"Are you fucking *insane*!" Queenie shouted, smacking the Sheikh on the head and then doing it again as she tried to control her panic. "You could have gotten us killed!"

"I would have died if I did not get to fuck you right now," said the Sheikh, grinning like a madman as he unbuckled his seatbelt and got out of the car, stumbling in the deep snow as he pulled his pants and underwear off his ankles.

Queenie stared in complete disbelief as the pantless Sheikh ran through the snow, circling the car and getting to her door. She tried to lock the door, but the safety measures had kicked in, which forced all the doors to unlock if there was an accident. The Sheikh pulled open her door, wrapped his arms around her so she wouldn't fall forward as he unbuckled her seatbelt. Then, as she laughed and screamed, he pulled her into the snow and pushed her down head-first, yanking down her jeans as she tried to playfully kick him away.

"You maniac!" she squealed as she felt the cold snow against her hips and pussy as the Sheikh grunted and growled as he pulled her jeans off and ripped her underwear right down the back seam. "You are seriously the most . . . oh, God, Bawaar! Oh, my fucking *God*!"

Her eyes rolled up in her head as she felt the Sheikh enter her from behind, the heat of his massive cock bringing out her own heat so quick she swore she heard the snow sizzle. And then he was fucking her, hard and with complete abandon, the two of them facing the midnight sun, Santa Claus on that billboard saying, "Have a Mushy Christmas!"

"Ya Allah!" he roared as he spread her rear cheeks, pushed his middle finger into her asshole, and twisted it around as he rammed into her so hard her entire body shuddered in rhythm. "Mush! Mush! *Mush*!"

Queenie almost choked with the mixture of laughter and arousal, heat and cold, the shock of the accident and the sheer joy of being taken so hard under the open skies where she'd grown up. She cried as she came, howled like an Arctic she-wolf as the Sheikh warmed her insides with his hot semen, pumping and growling like he was her animal mate out here in the Alaskan wilderness.

They came together in the eerie midnight sun for a long time, and only after the Sheikh collapsed on her back, pushing her face down into the snow, did Queenie realize they were almost buried in snow.

And so was their car.

24

"You do realize that your cock is to blame for this," Queenie said, crossing her arms over her breasts and shivering as she pressed on the accelerator and then looked back as the Sheikh tried to pull the rear wheels of the car back down so they could get enough traction to drive out of the ditch. "We're going to die out here because of your cock. I should have figured this was how I'd go. Dead because of a man's cock. I never believed Mama when she said 'Cock will be the death of you, child,' but here I am."

The Sheikh laughed, taking a break from his effort and strolling around to her window. "Did your mother really say that?"

"No, but it's something she mighta said," Queenie said. She looked around and frowned. "But seriously. I know you're strong and all, but you're not going to be able to tip a three ton car back from this angle. We need to call for help."

"How?" said the Sheikh, pulling out his phone and grimacing. "I still have no signal. How about you?"

Queenie looked at her phone for the hundredth time in the past hour and shook her head, and only when the Sheikh saw the glimmer of fear in her eyes did the seriousness of the situation begin to register. It was getting colder outside. They were miles from the last gas station, and miles from the next one. This was remote country, where Blue-Eyes's wife lived. People died out here.

The Sheikh took a breath and narrowed his eyes as he looked into the horizon. Then he turned and looked towards the road. They hadn't seen another car pass in either direction in almost two hours.

"There must be emergency callboxes out here," he said, keeping his voice calm,

"This far out? Yeah, but only every thirty miles or so."

"Which means the farthest I would have to walk is fifteen miles," said the Sheikh.

"Depends on the direction. I don't remember where the last call box was, so if we passed it like five miles ago and you choose to walk in the other direction, you'd have to go twenty-five miles! Besides, no one's walking anywhere! We're gonna stay put! Sooner or later a car will pass."

The Sheikh glanced at his Range Rover face-first in the snow. Then he turned towards the highway, which was a solid fifty yards away. Would a passing car see them from there? No.

"You stay in the car and keep warm," the Sheikh said. "There is water and some beef jerky in the backseat. I will wait by the highway and flag down the next vehicle."

Queenie frowned and bit her lip. "How far is Blue-Eyes's house?"

"Another fifty miles. Too far to walk," said the Sheikh. "This is our best option. Someone will see us."

"Eventually, but not before you freeze to death out there. We'll take shifts standing by the highway. I'll go first."

"No," said the Sheikh obstinately. "You will do as I say. Stay in the car."

"I have more body fat!" Queenie said, forcing a smile even though the Sheikh could see the panic building.

"I have more muscle. Also, I am in charge here."

Queenie laughed, pointing up at the sky. "That's who's in charge."

"God?" said the Sheikh.

"I meant the weather. But sure," Queenie said, her jaw tightening. Then suddenly she relaxed, her eyes going wide. "All right. I've got it. I should have thought of this earlier."

She got out of the car, and the Sheikh stared as she gathered their jackets, the water bottles, and the little food they had. She carried the supplies some distance away from the car, turning and looking back at him as she placed them on the ground.

"Get the toolbox out of the trunk in case we need something later. In fact, get anything we might need from the car." She stood straight and looked at him, a strange, almost excited glint in her eye. "Anything you don't want burned."

The Sheikh hesitated, and then he just grinned and did what she said. He grabbed the toolbox, a couple of blankets, the rubber floormats for added warmth and so they could camp out without getting wet. Then he just winked at her and stood back, watching his queen get to work.

He watched her as she dipped a dry rag into the gas tank, getting the edge of it damp with gasoline. Quickly she turned the rag over, pushing the other end into the gas tank.

"Now you've got your fuse," she said out loud like she was talking to herself. The Sheikh could see that she was enjoying this in a weird way, and he smiled when he realized she was as crazy as he was. As crazy as they all were. As crazy as the situation.

"No cigarette lighter in the car though," he said,

folding his arms across his chest and smiling. "And nothing in the emergency kit. I looked."

Queenie just narrowed her brown eyes at him and shrugged, reaching into her back pocket and pulling out a book of matches. "Old habits," she said winking as she struck two of them at once. "Stand back, love. Let the expert handle this."

The Sheikh stared in wonder as his woman carefully lit the edge of the rag, and he swore he saw pure, unadulterated delight light up her face as the flames caught. He almost ran over to pull her away from the car as she nonchalantly walked towards where he was standing, but he let her come to him at her own pace. This was her thing, he realized. She needed to do this.

The gas tank exploded just as Queenie got to him, and she slipped her arm in his as the car burst into glorious orange flame. Neither of them spoke, and finally the Sheikh put on his sunglasses, held her by the waist, and kissed her gently on the forehead as she stared into the fire . . . the fire which would keep them warm and also serve as a beacon to any passing cars. The fire which was going to save their lives.

"You want to borrow my sunglasses?" he said softly.

But Queenie just shook her head, her eyes riveted, wide open, the flames clearly reflected in her pupils. "Nope. I'm good."

25

"I'm good," Queenie said firmly as she looked at Mrs. Blue-Eyes and then over at Renita.

"You sure?" said Mrs. Blue-Eyes. "The tea is really good. Renita brought it over from the Middle-East." She turned to the Sheikh. "How about you? You like your tea sweet, right? Renita told me."

The Sheikh nodded, frowning slightly as he glanced at his ex-wife and then towards Queenie before forcing a smile and accepting the cup of steaming tea from the sandy-haired Mrs. Blue-Eyes.

Queenie tensed up as she watched the Sheikh blow on the liquid and then take a sip before smacking his lips. She'd considered stopping him from accepting

Mistletoe for the Sheikh

anything to eat and drink from these two witches, but then she'd reminded herself that the goal of this trip was forgiveness and resolution, not fighting and revenge. It was vengeance and obsession that had gotten them all into this, and forgiveness and peace was the only way out. It was the only way forward. It was the Christmas Way.

"So let me understand," said Renita, sipping her own tea and looking over at Bawaar and then Queenie. "How did the accident occur? Was there ice on the road?"

Queenie blinked as an image of the Sheikh running half-naked through the snow came to mind, and she almost laughed as she pictured showing Renita a video. She glanced over at Mrs. Blue-Eyes, studying her face carefully. She looked older than she was, Queenie could tell. Just like Blue-Eyes himself had looked like he'd aged dramatically since she'd last seen him. Was it the cancer? Was it stress? Was it his own obsessions that had taken their toll?

"What I'd like to understand is why you're here in the first place," Mrs. Blue-Eyes said.

"Why is *she* here?" Queenie snapped. Then she closed her eyes and took a breath. "I'm sorry. I'm still on edge. You know, maybe I will have a cup of that tea. Extra milk and sugar, please."

She waited while Mrs. Blue-Eyes poured the tea and Renita mixed in the milk and sugar. It was like a little ritual being shared by the three women, sort of a twisted version of the scene in the manger, with the three kings of orient paying a visit to the newborn that had brought them all together. She glanced over the Sheikh, wondering if he was Joseph in the analogy, if she herself was the Virgin Mary. Blasphemy aside, it kinda fit, didn't it? After all, she was going to be mother to a child that didn't come from her.

Stop it, she told herself as the tea warmed her insides. Just say what you came to say. You came to apologize. You came to forgive. Forgiveness asked and forgiveness given. That is the Christmas Spirit in a nutshell, isn't it? So just say it and go.

"I . . . I came to say . . ." Queenie began, blinking as she looked at Renita and then at Mrs. Blue-Eyes. "I just wanted to say that I'm—"

"I am sorry," Renita suddenly blurted out, her eyes going wide as she stared at Bawaar and then at Queenie. "That is why I am here! I am sorry I ever started this." She dried her eyes and then looked over at Mrs. Blue-Eyes. "But also not sorry, in a way. Because I have found a friend. We came together in a shared obsession for revenge, to make you hurt, to make you suffer in the same way we blamed you for our individual suffering. But—"

"But as my husband died, the last thing he said to me, just as his blue eyes closed for the last time, was that we both needed to let go, to forgive. To forgive each other. To forgive you. To forgive *you*, Queenie," said Mrs. Blue-Eyes.

"I don't understand," Queenie said, even though in a way she did. Blue-Eyes must have died on Christmas Day, and Queenie could feel that Christmas Spirit flowing through all of them, bringing it all to a close, wrapping it with a bow and a ribbon, red-and-green paper held firm by the emotional journeys of their intertwined lives.

"Yes, you do," said Mrs. Blue-Eyes. "My husband and I blamed you for all the troubles in our marriage, even though you were just the symptom, not the cause. The cause had nothing to do with you, and neither my husband nor I could acknowledge that. It seemed easier to blame you, to say that my man was seduced by a younger woman and turned his back on his family, to somehow focus all our energy on making you pay. We spent our life savings having you followed, waiting for you to find a man you loved so we could bring it all crashing down."

"After that public scene beneath the Mistletoe, she and her husband contacted me," Renita said. "We bonded. We became friends just in that first meeting. Perhaps it was that shared obsession with destroying someone, making someone suffer the way we believed we were made to suffer. We devised this plan to hurt you both, by dooming you to a life where your love could never manifest in marriage and family. When her husband died, we had Van Hosen's men transport the body to Europe, thinking we could implicate both of you in a murder investigation. It wouldn't have resulted in anything, but it would have destroyed Bawaar's image, made the new Sheikha look like an evil whore." Renita took a breath, her thin face widening slightly in a relaxed smile. "But in the process of all this madness we became friends. Real friends, Bawaar! It changed everything! I cannot explain it, but so much anger was released from my heart at the realization that I had a friend, someone who accepted me and all my twisted thoughts because she thinks the same way! A friend! Ya Allah, Bawaar! When have I ever had a friend?!"

"Never," said the Sheikh, and Queenie could see a flash of guilt in his eyes. "I should have been a better friend, even if I did not truly want to be your husband. I blamed you too, Renita. Blamed you for my own problems. I am sorry too, Renita."

Queenie took a breath as she fought back tears. It was twisted, but it did seem to fit that these women would bond over a shared obsession, a need for revenge—a need that somehow got met, strangely enough, by the reflection of themselves in each other! These were loners who'd suddenly found a BFF!

WTF, LOL, and Hallelujah, Queenie thought, almost laughing out loud as it made complete sense in a flash of joyful insight.

But then she thought of Blue-Eyes himself, and for the first time she felt sorry for him too. For the first time she forgave him too.

"But your husband . . . it couldn't have been coincidence that he died just in time for all of this," Queenie said. "How . . ."

"My husband has been living just one day away from death for almost two years now. He takes forty pills a day plus twice-daily dialysis to clean the toxins out of his system just to stay alive. The chemotherapy and cancer destroyed his organs. All he had to do was stop taking his pills and he would be gone within a day. So we chose Christmas Day. It seemed right, since you seemed to have found a man the night before, giving us a chance to complete our plan. A Christmas gift."

"So you had Van Hosen's men take the body to Europe and put it in that house . . ." said the Sheikh to Renita. "Ya Allah, you are a piece of work. I almost admire your mind and the way it twists. So what happened? Why did you not follow through on the plan?"

"You broke Van Hosen, got him to tell you where we were before we got the police to find the body," said Renita. "At that point I knew you would remove the body before the police would arrive, have your guards clean everything up. At the same time I had experienced that strange, almost miraculous change in outlook—and so had Mrs. Blue-Eyes after her husband's dying request. So we decided it was over, and I called my new friend and told her I was coming over for the holidays. Up to the North Pole, where Santa Claus lives! What better place to give birth to my child!"

Queenie's heart jumped when she heard Renita mention the child. But it was almost a leap of joy—not for anyone else but for the unborn child itself! Yes, she was committed to raising the child herself if Renita didn't want it, but of course it would be better if the mother did indeed want her child, right?

"Your child," said the Sheikh softly. "So you are really pregnant?"

"Yes," Renita said softly. "I thought it was a cruel joke that after so many years, it only happened after we separated."

"Perhaps that's *why* it happened," Queenie said, frowning as she felt the Spirit of Christmas as if it were a real thing in the room with them. "Perhaps although you weren't meant to be together, you were meant to have a child. Because if not for that child, none of this would have manifested, right? We'd all still be living our lives with anger in our hearts, revenge on our minds, obsessing about being insulted by others, taking delight in blaming others for what was wrong in our own lives!" She smiled and shook her head as the tears came. "You know, we forget sometimes that Christmas began because a child was born. It's all about a child. It's all about family."

"And this child will have a bigger family than it ever imagined," said Renita, raising her teacup and smiling as she locked arms with her new BFF.

"Perhaps a bigger family than it ever *wants*," said the Sheikh, half under his breath. "Three mothers? Ya Allah, I certainly hope it is a girl."

Queenie raised an eyebrow. "Really? You want to live the rest of your life answering to four women again? A real Mama's boy, right?"

The Sheikh turned bright red as all the women laughed, and finally he joined in as well. But not before giving Queenie a look that was for her and her alone. A look that reminded her that he was king, he was Sheikh, he was the alpha animal. He might keep his mouth shut now and join the laughter of the women, but when they were alone he would show her that side of him that no one else had seen, no one else would understand, no one else would accept.

Acceptance, forgiveness, understanding, Queenie thought as she raised her own teacup and smiled, wondering if it was just her imagination or did the swirling steam really look like a jolly, white-bearded man winking and saying, "Have a Mushy Christmas!"

Have a Mushy Christmas, everyone.

Always and forever.

∞

EPILOGUE
<u>SEPTEMBER 25 OF THE NEW YEAR</u>

"**W**hat do we name her?" said the Sheikh.

Queenie thought for a moment. She counted back nine months just to be sure, smiling at her newborn daughter before looking up into the Sheikh's eyes.

"Christmas," she said. "We'll name her Christmas."

∞

May your Christmas be as mushy as this novel, my lovely romance fans!
Love, Anna.
∞

From Annabelle Winters

Thanks for reading.

Join my private list at **annabellewinters.com/join** to get steamy epilogues, exclusive scenes with side characters, and a chance to join my advance review team.

And do write to me at **mail@annabellewinters.com** anytime. I really like hearing from you.

Love,
Anna.

Made in the USA
San Bernardino, CA
15 January 2020